Little Black E

Volume 2
Mr. Oh

STREET LITERATURE

Published by Street Literature. All rights reserved. Without limiting the rights under copyright reserved above. No part of this book may be reproduced, stored in or introduced into a retrieval system, or transmitted, in any form, or by any means (electronic, mechanical, photocopying, recording, or otherwise), without prior written consent from both the author, and Street Literature, except brief quotes used in reviews.

Little Black Book Volume 2
Copyright © 2012 Street Literature
Written by: Mr. Oh
Cover Artwork: Shannon Walters

ISBN-13: 978-1489580900
ISBN-10: 1489580905

Follow Street Literature
Web: www.streetliterature.co.uk

Follow the Author
Twitter: www.twitter.com/mrohyes
Facebook: www.facebook.com/StreetLiteratureBooks

Follow Shannon
Web: www.shannonwalters.com

ACKNOWLEDGMENTS

Thank you to all who bought, borrowed, enjoyed or read Little Black Book volume 1 and I hope you enjoy the next installment.

Mr. Oh

DEDICATION

Still dedicated to London and the stories that she inspires.
Love you London

Mr. Oh

CONTENTS

- STREET LITERATURE 3
- ACKNOWLEDGMENTS 5
- DEDICATION 7
- CONTENTS 9
- The Meeting 11
- Miles & Melissa 15
- Escaping Temptation 39
- Passion Play 57
- Do Me Right 61
- Honouree's Reward 77
- Marcus and the Truth 89
- Office Tales 103
- Escaping Temptation 125
- Ladies Nite 143
- Foot Soles & Pantyhoes 167
- Your Chair 203
- Moody Blue 207

The Meeting

Words cannot describe
How I feel when your in my sight
Don't be worried about tonight
Breakfast in the AM and you'll be alright

See the world spins on an axis
And the one and only fact is
I know your body better than you do
There to touch
That spot tickles
Keep my hands away from that giggly middle
Smile below your sternum likes a flick just a little

10 minute flow and your the Nile in my bedroom
And all this takes place
With a smile on your face
Notice the evil smirk, you ain't got no time to waste
Fiddling with ya fingers, biting on your lip
You know how much I really love that shit

Drink your juice and be easy with me
Relax yourself and let your soul be free
Protect your everything with one almighty squeeze
I'm the waiter tonight and I aim to please
Walk closer but slowly, pigeon steps only
Make it last as long as possible
But don't be mad when tomorrow your drowsy
Seriously

I'm supplying and delivering
And this is just the first part
Of our initial meeting...

Miles & Melissa

The sun fell from the sky like a missile from a fighter jet. Night covered the city like a cloak, causing the fearful to hide in their places of refuge but for those who didn't fear, the night was their time.

A group of people walking past waiting traffic; laughing, bussing joke, pointing and generally having a nice time, were on their way out. The leader of the group, Melissa, was celebrating her 27nd birthday and decided that, because she didn't do anything for her 26th, she would make this year a big one.

"Come on you lot, lets go, the club ain't gonna wait."

Her weave looked as fresh as a L'Oreal advert and bobbed perfectly to her head. Her slim, slender body was covered by an ankle- length dress that mirrored every curve of her body. The Nefertiti face on the front was slim over her six-pack stomach and stuck out over her behind. And if you looked carefully, you could see her thong as the warm autumn breeze nipped at her sparkly Primark heels.

Her crew for the night, a mix of men and women, were a collection of old friends, new friends, relatives, their friends and some unknowns.

Her good friend Apollo was dancing and walking to an imaginary beat and her media lecturer Miss Charlery was talking to her sister.

Though Melissa was content with the people who came out to celebrate her born day, there was one person she was particularly looking forward to seeing.

She felt they shared a special bond that no one could infiltrate and they became good friends because of it but never took it to that next level, even though they both felt it.
But he wasn't here yet; he was supposed to meet her inside the club.

Miles.

Melissa couldn't wait to see him again. They hadn't seen each other since the last day of Miles' employment at JD Sports when they walked home, as they usually did, when they were on shift together.

The wind blew just like tonight and Miles and Melissa leisurely strolled through Wood Green before they both turned and went their separate ways. As they reached the cross-roads that separated them many times before, Melissa turned to Miles to say her goodbye but Miles was already in her face, close enough to suck the breath out of her.

"Miles, I don't think..."

Was all she managed to say before Miles pulled her close and kissed her with all the passion of a highly anticipated first time kiss. He wrapped his arms around her back, enclosing her in his warmth and made sure that she felt his protective grip. Melissa's slow response was not because she didn't want to kiss him (she had dreamed about it many times before and even masturbated at the thought) she just never had the guts.

Now it was happening so fast, and it felt the way she thought it would.

His warm lips were slightly moist and he tilted his head softly to the right and stroked her chin with his gloved hand.

Once or twice, Melissa opened her eyes and made sure that he didn't have his eyes open, a superstition she held onto.

Eyes closed, YES, Melissa thought.

She took her arms and wrapped them around his neck, making her moan in the kiss. Miles responded by hugging her tighter.

When they eventually broke, Miles looked into Melissa's honey brown eyes and opened his mouth and uttered words that would never leave her heart.

"If this is the first and last time I kiss you, I'll know I've tasted love."

Melissa's body almost melted as she looked back into Miles' eyes, which were so sexy that, if there was a semi-lit alley close by, she would drag him into it.

And hump the hell out of him.

Miles kissed her again, his lips slipping over hers softly, and then walked off without saying goodbye. This intrigued Melissa and made her wonder what the hell he was thinking.

She wanted to shout his name and run to him on some soap-opera tip but she was still shocked that he was still walking away.

After such a delicious kiss, Melissa was feeling her lips as she watched him get smaller in the distance. Miles strolled with his music in his ears and Melissa watched him disappear around a corner and out of her life.

With the thought of the kiss on her mind, Melissa couldn't wait to see Miles again. She wasn't sure what she would do when she saw him but she knew that he wasn't just going to walk away from her again.

The club was packed to the brim with people, some dancing, some profiling on the sidelines like train-spotters watching trains pass them by. But Melissa and her entourage decided that that wasn't gonna fly.
Once they had their jackets in the cloakroom, they took a space on the dance floor and made room for themselves and waved their hands in the air, like they just didn't care.

By the middle of the evening, Melissa looked over her shoulders so many times her neck started to ache. She was looking for Miles' plaited head to bob through the crowd and find her but he wasn't here yet and if he was then he was being evil and not showing himself.

"He'll be here," Melissa's sister Janae said.

"Who?" Melissa answered, trying to act oblivious to what her sister was talking about.

"Okay then," Janae winked as she swept the floor with her feet, Energy God-style.

The club was well and truly road blocked by the time Melissa and her crew stopped dancing. The music came to an abrupt end and the DJ took to the mic.

"Send a shout out to Melissa celebrating her 27th birthday. Don't worry, he'll park himself right behind you darling, hold tight everyone inside..."

Her crew raised their arms to let the club know where the birthday girl was hiding her face. Through an embarrassed smile, Melissa put her arms in the air and screamed. She was extra excited because she knew that Miles here too.
When the DJ said that he would 'park' himself behind her, Melissa knew.

Park.

The personal joke between the two of them they created during one of their boring days hidden in the stockroom, labelling boxes of Air Max 90s.

To park was to take your nipple and put it in your partner's belly button. The sensation, they discussed, must've felt strange but somehow sexual.

Melissa pivoted on her feet and searched the club for a familiar part of his face or clothes.
But still no Miles.
The DJ began the music again with Musiq Soulchild's Sunny Days. This song pissed Melissa off as it was from the album that Miles bought for her way back when. She read between the lines, between each groove and danced while scanning the room for him.

The next song mixed in slowly and Melissa, now half way onto her desired drunken level with a sixth glass of champagne, was well into a good zone. Her dress moved with each twist of her body and became her skin at times as her nipples poked out from the cool breeze of the air conditioning.
Before she could poke them out, she looked down at her ankles and thought she saw two hands circling her calf muscles, working their way up. Making sure she wasn't hallucinating, she waited until they got past her knees before she decided that they were real hands.
Miles caught her as she spun to face him and enveloped her in his arms, while her crew and the music continued in their background. His tall frame and distinctively sharp features made him a chocolate God, but he was so humble and insecure that he became more attractive with it.

"Did you say happy birthday to me on the record up there...with the JD...I mean the DJ?" Melissa's slurred speech and mixed words showed that she was a bit tipsy but not fully drunk.
"Yeah I did..."
And with that, Miles and Melissa joined together and stayed stuck like weave and glue.
Every genre of music the DJ dared to play was a new challenge for them to slow grind to.
Forehead-to-forehead, their eyes watching the movements of their hips, imagining the lower connection without any clothes between them.
They stared each other in the eyes and came dangerously close to kissing but never did. The tease was more delicious than the delivery.
Miles enjoyed the tease because he had a plan and Melissa

didn't because she did not want to kiss in front of Janae, who was dancing with the Apollo, Miss Charlery and the rest of her birthday crew. But she didn't plan to be with her sister ALL night.

Several injured high-heeled feet later, the lights came on, filling the room with reality and actuality. People dancing together looked at each other to see if the light would reveal a dog dancing partner. Many people had their phones out and were swapping numbers; other couples were standing and talking with grins, while security was telling everyone, 'you don't have to go home but you have to fuck off'.

Melissa and crew all met outside just left of the clubs huge double doors. Melissa held onto Miles' hand, as not to lose him.

Not again.

As her crew dispersed, going their own ways to get home, Melissa spoke to Janae, still holding Miles' hand. He apologetically interrupted their conversation.

"Sorry ladies but my ride is here."

A purple Hummer limousine pulled up on the other side of the road and the driver descended and held the back door open.

Miles waved.

"So make sure she gets home okay, you hear me?" Janae said to Miles.

"What?!" Melissa shrieked.

"Look, you two have a lot of catching up to do and if Miles has a limo then he can spend some time with you before you go home, right MILES?"

Janae said his name as if to make sure he got the point.
He did.

"Shall we? Your carriage awaits."

"You okay to get home?" Melissa said, swaying and tipsily two-stepping in her heels.

"Sure, I'll get a cab; I've seen my friend Osvaldo and he's going the same way as me so we'll share one. Go on!"

With that said and agreed, Melissa hugged Miles' mid-section and they careful crossed the busy street and into the limousine.

Soft lighting and Erykah Badu's Window Seat harmonising made the cream decor interior all too sexy. First in with her mouth open, Melissa held her dress as so not to trip on it as she entered, giving Miles a sight of her thigh as he followed behind.

"Where to?" the driver asked from the front seat.

"Royston, could you take us for a drive around London?" Miles looked at Melissa and smiled as he saw the intention in her eyes.

The limousine pulled out and began to travel through the late night/early morning traffic, turning softly and braking even softer.

Staring at her for a long moment, Miles said nothing. She was still gazing at the interior, lost in how sexy everything was. Spot lights, sheets lights wrapped around window frames and a bottle of champagne on ice.

"So how have you been?" Miles began the small talk.

Melissa was staring all around, amazed at the perfection of the limousine like it was the carriage to heaven. She didn't think her first time in a limo would be with Miles but now she was here, she was struck dumb.

"Look, I'm a little pre-tipsy..."

"PRE-tipsy?" Miles asked.

"Yeah, pre-tipsy. When your touched but not tipsy. Oh YEAH... where's my present?" Melissa sat up as she looked at Miles from her seat.

She folded one of her legs in the space between them and raised her dress to expose her thigh.

Miles tried his best not to look into dark abyss between her legs but the more she made herself comfortable, the more he saw.

He leaned across and picked up the bottle of champagne.

"I know you're already a little tipsy so you may not be able for this."

She scanned the bottle, acting like she knew what it was, "Yeah, pop that."

She watched him unwrap the foil, watching his fingers. The way they were cautious when they got to the cork.

It popped with the first touch and a small stream of bubbles fell to the floor.

Melissa planned to slow sip her first glass, otherwise the bubbles would go straight to her head, as always, and she would be throwing up sooner rather than later.

Pouring two glasses, Miles handed her one and they clinked.

"So, what do you think your present is?" Miles played dumb a little bit more.

"One of your stories of course. I wanted you to write me a story of my own."

Miles smiled then looked at Melissa as she looked back. He got up from his seat and scooted closer. Melissa's heart jumped, thinking he was going to kiss her.

As Miles continued to move forward, he stopped to put his drink down. Suddenly the partition between them and the driver drew up until it closed.

Just like in the movies, Melissa thought.

As she turned her head, Miles was there again to steal her breath. She turned into his lips and he kissed her.

He did it AGAIN.

She couldn't believe he managed to get into her personal space without her feeling him there. She remembered how she felt when he did it the first time, when it was their last time. But this time, it was much more sensual.

Miles sat down beside Melissa and leaned over as she leaned backwards, carefully putting her drink down as she went. He followed her with his lips and they locked onto each other.

Her initial hum was a reaction to the feel of his lips and the taste of champagne on his breath.

Their lips locked perfectly on each other and at times, Miles dropped his lips and sucked both of her lips individually. Melissa seemed to like it more when he sucked her bottom lip, so Miles concentrated.

"So you want a story do you? Okay."

"Yeah... tell me a story," Melissa's breathing was laboured and heavy.

"Okay, let's see...well let's start in a bedroom with a man and woman. The woman is lying down and the man is stroking her body softly."

As Miles spoke, he took his left hand and rubbed it up and down her body so softly that it was like he wasn't touching her at all. Melissa closed her eyes and inhaled deeply as Miles continued talking and caressing.

"Then he kisses her on her neck and shoulders..."

Melissa was breathing hard as Miles spoke but as he followed his words with his mouth, she grabbed the back of his head and ran her hands through his half cornrow, half twisted hair.

He was making her hungrier with each word that oozed from

his lips.

"Then what..." Melissa begged.

"The man moves down to her stomach and kisses around her navel, making sure that he kisses every part..."

With her dress still on, Melissa could feel Miles' lips over her stomach.

She really wanted to be OUTSIDE the dress with Miles INSIDE her.

"What's his name?" Melissa asked, breathless.

"Erm... Marcus?"

She looked at him. "Who?"

"Miles?"

"Yeah, I like Miles better... anyway, what is MILES doing now?"

"Then the woman begins to moan as the Miles makes his kisses get lower and lower and his tongue makes a trail from her belly button down her thighs and round her..."

Melissa screamed and inhaled at the same time, which surprised Miles but didn't stop him. Though she had a dress and thong on, Miles softly chewed on where he imagined her clit would be. He was right, judging from Melissa's reaction.

He knew that this was where he could now get a little more personal and daring with the story.

Taking off his shirt and rolling her dress from her ankles all the way up her body, Miles watched Melissa's staggered breathing as her body came to light in London's illuminated West End.

Look at my thighs, I need to step up my squat game.
What a flabby belly, I'll do more sit-ups in the morning.

"...Then Miles strokes her breasts and kisses them then parks with her too..."

Melissa smiled drunkenly as she felt Miles poke and park his nipple in her belly button. Her bra was no trouble, as Miles unhooked all clasps with one hand.

"Impressive," Melissa whispered to herself as her nipples stood in anticipation.

With her bra at her feet, Miles circled each breast with his tongue, slow and concentrated, swapping from sucking to licking to flicking to nibbling.

Melissa giggled as he put a finger in his mouth, moistened it then put it on his nipple which slipped in and out of her belly button.

"What?" Miles asked, meeting her smile.

"You park really well," Melissa said through her laugh.

"Thank you, I had a good driving instructor."

Miles' head disappeared beyond Melissa's eyesight but she could definitely feel what he was saying.

His hands crept up the sides of her body and she could feel herself giving him more permission.

Her body shuddered at the feeling of his hands on her naked skin and, as she raised her head to watch what he would do next, she was just in time to see her thong slide to the left.

She tried to hold her head up but found that Miles knew how to control her from his first lick between her lips.

With his eyes closed, glasses off and long shake of his hair, Melissa thought she saw God between her thighs.

Trying to think, Melissa was distracted as Miles used his nipple technique of switching from sucking to licking to flicking to nibbling on her clitoris, which had now inflamed to twice its previous size.

Melissa kept her hands locked around Miles' head and began to pull him deeper into her pussy. But not too hard, she didn't want to kill him.

And at that moment, she felt like she could suffocate him and get over the guilt in her orgasm.

At times, she thought she was stopping his breathing but the feeling was so good that she had to have him deeper.

"You okay up there?" Miles asked.

"Just fine, just fine," Melissa answered. "You okay? I'm not suffocating you am I?"

"Do I care?" Miles replied with a long slurp.

The sound of London at night became more than a background sound as a slight breeze licked them.

With her hands gripping his skull, Melissa squinted through the pleasure to see that her wandering foot was resting comfortably on the door handle.

"OH MY FUCKING... SHIT... ALL OF IT..."

Melissa threw her head far back and ran her hand through her hair as she felt Miles' tongue continue its journey inside her.

Due to the fact that Melissa attracted men who didn't go down, it had been a real REAL long time for her. Just experiencing his initial licks gave her the mental note to get some more head in her life.

Taking her leg and locking it against the roof of the limo, Melissa let her voice out as she felt heat rising in her tight stomach as the limo stopped at a set of traffic lights.

"Oh shit, look at them in there... REH... Ah fam, he's yamming the pum pum... Wow, wish my man would do me like that..."

Miles was far enough inside her that he couldn't hear the voices behind him but Melissa opened her eyes and noticed she had opened the window all the way down with her foot, giving them an audience.

"Miles, the windows... oh shit... Miles stop for a minute, the window is open. People can see us!"

Keeping his head buried in her crotch, while she frantically tried to close the window and cover her face at the same time, Miles spoke in a low voice.

"Let them watch..."

"No, too many perverted people out there!"

"You should worry about the perverted person down here."

And with that Melissa tried to close the window with her foot. She couldn't recreate the same action that caused it to open and Miles turned back to her slippery self.

Encircling her clitoris with his lips, Miles slowly licked up and down. His tongue made a continual slurp as her lips parted. While she tried to get up and reach for the window, Miles pushed her down and she screeched.

She wanted to see if anyone was looking as she felt the limo pull away from the lights but Miles was doing something real good.

The vehicle pulled away from whoops, whistles and shouts of encouragement from the watching crowd.

Melissa dropped back and revelled in the soft touch Miles used to spread her lips apart, while using his fingers to run across her inner thigh.

Looking back, Miles closed the window. "Now you can relax."

Melissa pulled him up on top of her and kissed him full on the lips. Her sugar was electricity for their kiss and they scoffed and slurped, both hungry to get more.

Breaking from their kiss, Melissa held Miles' head and looked him in his eyes, so sexy and brown, with her syrup scent filling the space between them.

"Miles, I've missed you so much! Ever since that day when you just walked off, I've been waiting for you to call me."

"I would've called you but THAT phone with your number in it was stolen from my friend's car time ago one night when we went raving."

Melissa's eyes broadened as she heard Miles' revelation. At one point, she actually began to resent him for not calling her, thinking he wasn't interested.

Maybe he's telling the truth, maybe he isn't but considering what he just did to my pussy I don't care, Melissa thought.

"Then I heard about your party, so I thought I'd come."

"It's nice to see you though. A bit late to say that considering I can taste me on your face but at least I'm polite." Melissa said stroking the contours of his face, taking him all in with her fingers.

"Thank you for coming too."

"But I didn't..."

"You WILL."

In between each break of their conversation, they kissed, stroked, hugged and just admired each other's beauty. The movement of the limo made them jerk softly against the leather seats.

Melissa closed her eyes and dropped her head as if sleep suddenly attacked. Her lengthy lashes shot open suddenly, just as Miles was about to ask her what was wrong.

"Miles, I want you to fuck me, right now!"

The look of astonishment on Miles' face was nothing compared to the instant erection that shot up from his boxers. Melissa dropped her head and saw it pop up like toast. She wanted to pop it into her mouth and try something new.

What type of thought is that, Melissa thought as the notion of performing oral sex on ANYONE surprised the hell out of her. But it had entered her head nonetheless.

Melissa was one of those ladies who wasn't interested in giving any man a blowjob, head or whatever it was called. It was nasty to her. She didn't see the pleasure women gained from having a man's penis poking around the inside of their mouths. Her girlfriends would tell stories of their dick-sucking antics and she would zone out, refusing to acknowledge such pleasure existed.

But right here, right now, Melissa could understand the urge.

It was a low powerful surge that grew inside her as soon as Miles' representative popped out to say hello.

Melted chocolate brown, with an equal measure of length and girth, was warm in her hand.

She let it dance between her fingers and move to her soft touch.

"But I haven't finished my story..."
"Well finish it NOW!"

Melissa charged Miles, knocking him over and onto his back flat on the leather sofa. Her kiss was charged with so much passion that Miles' erection became painful, as if the flesh of his dick was trying to break through the skin.

The heat from her thighs replaced the breeze that had previously occupied the limo. Her slender body, thick thighs and monster ass were out of her dress and, naked, he imagined she was the answer to all questions.

Miles ran his hands over her entire body as they kissed and he drew a condom from his jeans pocket, which were slung on the floor of the limo.

Rip, unravel, wrap, ready.

Miles looked at Melissa, who was now naked and hot, with a thin coating of perspiration on her forehead.

Apparently it was easier to get the dress on than it was to get the dress off and she had a little moment of frustration as she wrestled her way out.

"Ready?" Miles asked.
"Was ready before you were!"

The pair moved over to the sofa on the other side of the limo, which was longer and far away from any windows that may open, by accident. The lights seem to dim softly as if the driver knew that they were getting ready to play the proper game.

Frank McComb's Cupid's Arrow sang in the limo as Miles and Melissa discarded any obstructions.

Putting himself down first, Miles took his dick and stood it up as Melissa crouched over then climbed on top, slowly.

They shared a moment, before he slipped in. Their eyes locked

and it was as if they both stopped breathing.
She grinned before he did.

Easing herself down and nearly blacking out, Melissa couldn't understand how his dick was fuller than it first appeared when she had it in her hand. He slipped inside faster than she anticipated and she had to raise up off him, real quick.

Their eyes met in a moment of 'that's a lot of dick'. They smiled and she ran a finger over his lips before kissing him.

His lips were sex to her, the way they accommodated her lips, warmed them up right nice and made the regrowth on the back of her neck stand up.

By the time she sat down fully, slowly this time, Melissa didn't want to get up. Miles was so deep inside her that she thought she could feel him behind her nipples.

"NO, NO, don't do that... please don't move yet."

Melissa opened her eyes wide and stared Miles down as he began to pump himself further inside her. He stayed still and looked up at Melissa, who now held her breasts and lifted herself up slowly then put herself down just as slow. Her eyes were closed and her head tilted back as she gradually picked up speed and began to ride Miles like the limo they were cruising in.

Miles grabbed her ass and tried to speed her down, as she rubbed down on him like she was trying to erase him from existence. No longer pumping up and down, she was moving back and forth, making his dick move all around.

"Suck them please..."

Melissa put her hands behind Miles' neck and hoisted him up to the same level as her breasts, slipping her lefty into his mouth. Never one to turn down a request, Miles extended his tongue and wrapped it around her nipple.

The sound she made told him that his tongue was the perfect sauce for her meal as she let her head fall back again. Melissa began bouncing up and down; secreting with each push.

"Miles... stop me... PLEASSSSSSE... I don't want to come yet..."

"Shhh...you come when you want..."

Miles was enjoying the fact that Melissa was bouncing up and down so easily, which meant she was so wet that the movement wasn't restrictive at all.

"OH SHIT, MILES...I'M GONNA COME...HELP ME..."

Grabbing her ass cheeks roughly, Miles bounced her up and

down faster than she was already bouncing. Her neck shone in his face and he put his lips to it, her nipples bouncing against his chest.

"MILES... I'M COMING... KEEP DOING THAT..."

In an almighty scream, and a timely jerk from the limousine, Melissa pumped herself a few times then pushed her pussy down onto Miles' dick and stayed right there, sucking air through her teeth.

It was like musical statues and the music stopped.

She wrapped her arms around his neck and held on for dear life as her pussy gripped his dick. With each pulse, she sucked more air through her teeth.

Her hands started around his neck, across his shoulders, down his back, along his arms and back again.

Birthday orgasmmmm...

After a minute of her throbs, Miles spoke.

"You okay?"

"I can't remember the last time someone made me make that noise. It's been a while. In fact, I don't even think I've ever felt like that before."

"Is that a good thing?"

"Oh hell yeah... definitely..."

"Good... very good!" Miles smiled.

"Well... that only leaves you now!" Melissa clambered down from Miles' lap and sat adjacent from him with her legs spread-eagle.

"What'd you mean?!"

"I've arrived, now it's your turn!"

The limo stopped and the partition that separated the driver and the naked pair vibrated with a tap tap tap. Melissa panicked and scrambled for her clothes, trying to dress as well as move away from the partition at the same time. Miles calmed her down and got close enough to the partition that the driver wouldn't be able to see anything else.

As it slid open, Miles looked out the blackened window and realised they were in a park

"I thought that you two would like to sit in the park for a

while," Royston said.

"Oh, erm... no thank you."

"I meant chill out in the car. I'm gonna go and smoke a spliff, you two cool?"

"We're cool. Gwarn and do ya thing."

The partition slid back and Miles looked at Melissa, who had covered herself with her dress.

The door slammed as Miles snatched her dress away from her and smiled at the naked beauty in front of him. She smiled back and moved towards him, ready to begin what they halted.

"Do you like stars?" Melissa asked.

"Stars?"

"Yeah, you know like stars in the sky?"

Miles grinned. "They're alright. You know, they just chill out in the sky. Look good on a clear night."

"Like tonight."

Melissa looked up at the sunroof, which looked the size of the skylight in her office.

"Does that work?"

"I haven't tried it to be honest. Let's see."

He pressed a button and the sunroof whirred open, exposing a deep blue blanket of diamonds lights.

"Isn't that nice?" she said, looking up and laying her head on his shoulder.

"That IS nice, let's have a look."

Miles straightened her head before standing up and staring at the sky through the open sunroof, snapping off the condom at the same time.

The night air had warmed considerably and his torso basked in the temperature change.

"I'm just gonna put my bra on."

"NO, come and enjoy it the way you are." Miles replied looking down. "It's ya barfday."

Omar's In The Morning played like a theme song as she reached for her glass of champagne.

Feeling more sober than she did when she first got into the limo, Melissa tilted her head back and downed the rest of her drink.

She winced as the bubbles went straight to her head. Weaving and wining in her seat, she put her hands on the seat to steady herself through the sea of woozy her head was dancing on.

Are you hungry baby, can I fix you something, run a bath for you, some soap and loving, there's no place I'd rather be, then right here, right now, with you...

Omar sang.

When her head had returned to the dry land of stability, she opened her eyes to Miles' thigh in front of her.

She thought he played some kind of sport because his thigh looked the size of a tree stump. A nice chocolate tree stump with a semi-branch protruding.

Melissa felt that low urge to suck his dick again. She felt it earlier but it hit stronger and harder this time as he stared at the night sky.

"There are SO many stars up here. Come and look," Miles said.

"Hold on, I'm just getting my drink," she lied in reply.

She slid round the sofas until she was sitting directly in front of his dick.

It was resting between his thighs as he gazed above. She turned her head to the left and just looked at it.

Not impressed that the first time she thought about sucking a dick had to be with quite a large one.

Thinking back to all the head horror stories she had to endure, she was glad she actually listened.

Miles was still gazing at the stars above as Melissa stared, undecided at which angle to start from.

She was back and forth, trying to not to come off like the rookie she was.

Secretly, she DID watch the odd Lethal Lipps video online, just to see what all the fuss was about.

In theory, the act still disgusted her but she was still enthralled by her performances.

Maybe this was why.

Melissa sighed heavily, blinked hard, then opened her mouth and took him up to the middle of his shaft. The sensation instantly felt odd. It felt like an oversized sausage that she couldn't bite. Sliding her lips back, she closed her eyes and thought of her friends and the advice they had given her about sucking dick.

She looked up to see Miles looking down at her. Smiling back at him, she tried the head turn thing her girls swore by, also trying to make his dick wet in her mouth, instead of swallowing the saliva down.

His pleasured face was reassurance that her girls weren't just shit talkers.

She felt excited. Her mouth watered as she straightened her head.

Suddenly, she took a small sip of her refilled champagne and squirted it through her teeth onto his dick.

"WHOA SHIT... WHAT..."

"Just shut up up there, I'm doing something," Melissa replied.

Her answer was more dismissive than anything else, in fact his reaction was distracting her away from the way his dick was rising in front of her eyes.

Melissa approached from the left but hesitated. She was sucking back saliva that was building in her mouth. Her tongue was active in desire as it moistened her lips.

She scowled and stared the dick down.

Her lips parted in front of him and she cautiously approached.

"Look at the sky," she said.

"I'd rather watch you," he replied, all sweet boy-ish.

"It's MY birthday and you have to do what I say."

With his eyes up towards the gleaming night sky, Melissa looked back to his dick and gave it another kiss. She returned with a second kiss and slipped his head into her mouth.

Deeper than before with a slight gag.

Straight out though. She wasn't ready for a full deepthroat.

Result, Melissa thought.

Her lips felt the need to wrap around his hardness and squeeze as he withdrew from her mouth. That felt like the right thing to do.

Her nipples hardened as she stared at his dick, now shining from the wetness of her mouth.

She hiccuped and took a swig of her drink then burped.

Holding him with one hand, she turned his dick to the left and kissed it's length, sliding her lips up and down. She did the same to the right side, then kissed it again, this time daring to take him a little bit deeper.

She winced and squinted as she felt him reach the back of her teeth. Her gag reflex kicked in and she coughed on his dick, taking him out.

"You okay?" Miles asked, trying to look down.

"Stars bredrin," Melissa replied, gulping more libation.

Holding his dick strong, she stared at it as if it was late on a payment.

She was tight with the grip as she watched and waited. She wanted him to droop.

The process began and his dick wilted from a strong Tyrese presence to a small Carlton Banks stature.

With his head dropping, she approached it and slid it into her mouth, with no kiss. This time she wanted him in her mouth. She wanted to feel him grow.

Using her tongue to guide him deeper, Melissa ran her tongue up and down his shrunken member.

His response was instant and he filled her mouth within seconds. She leaned back to take less then began to suck him slowly.

Miles slapped the roof of the limo and made her jump, but she was INTO the flow of what she was doing. And she was sweet on the fact that she was liking what she was doing.

Whatever it was, she was feeling all of it.

Her eyes closed all by themselves and she worked what she knew, remembered and learned.

All of it making total sense.

With Miles' dick in her mouth, Melissa let go of her presumptions and went for it.

His hips started to pump into her mouth and she worked with his rhythm as J Dilla's Think Twice played.

Miles dick slipped out of her mouth and he sat down next to her.

"I can't take any more of that, you mad?" Miles said, heavy breathing.

"You likes, you likes, you likes?"

"That's SOME head game you got there, who trained you? Lethal, Lacey, Ayana, Italia?"

"Who are they?"

Miles giggled, "No one, they just know about good head and THAT is good head."

She opened her mouth to say something but she decided not to. The compliment was served. She had also broken a personal barrier and was proud to say that she liked it and was, apparently, good at it.

"Close your eyes."
"What?" Miles asked.
"Close your eyes, I wanna do something."
"What can't you do with my eyes open?"
"Oi Miles, Nike?"
"Just do it... alright fine."

Using his hands as comedic blindfolds, Miles closed AND covered his eyes with his hands. Making sure he didn't peek, he listened as the leather of the limo creaked and squeaked, meaning that Melissa was moving around doing something.

"Can I open them yet?"
"Yes!"

Dropping his hands and opening his eyes, Miles looked forward and saw nothing but ass in his face. Melissa was bent over, ready and waiting for him to take his position behind her.

Wasting no time, he got up, strapped up again and held onto her hips as he lined up himself with her pussy, slowly pushing his dick inside her.

Her earlier orgasm caused her to become a leaky tap. As he withdrew, he looked down and saw his dick glisten and shine with juice.

Miles put his hand in the middle of her back and made her bend over more so the only thing in the air was her ass.

Face down, ass up huh?

Slowly building up, Miles reached round and softly massaged her clit, which was still sensitive.

"OHHH... SSSHHHIIITTT..."

The words shook out of her mouth as she began backing her ass onto him. She felt herself losing control and began moaning again.

The rhythm was instantly quick, no build up.

"TAKE THAT... OOHH... SHIT... YES... THAT'S IT..."

Miles could also feel himself losing control but he couldn't let himself lose that much control. Like ALL men, he felt that if he kept quiet then it would show that he could control himself, thus making himself look like THE MAN!

But he couldn't hold on.

"I'm gonna come..." Miles said deeply.

"COME MILES... pleaseeeeeee..." Melissa begged.

As the limo rocked, Miles' pumping got faster and faster until he made one penultimate surge into Melissa's pussy. His cream seed pumped into the plastic guardian, which drove Melissa crazy as she could feel the heat from his sperm filling her walls, but going nowhere.

"I'M GONNA..."

As quickly as she spoke, Melissa collapsed onto her stomach and lay completely still, slipping him out. Miles unrolled the condom and tied the end, making sure no errant runners escaped.

He whipped it out of the sunroof into the abyss of the park to be found by a squirrel later on.

Melissa was still lying on her stomach and was softly humming to herself. She sounded like a computer game at first but she got louder and louder until Miles recognised it as Jill Scott's Is It the Way.

Miles loved that song.

He lay across from her and stared into her eyes, humming with her until the driver got back into the Hummer and started it up again.

Flicking back a panel in the door, Miles pulled out an iPod and searched until he found the song.

She sighed as her arms wrapped around him. He nestled his face in her neck and they sang to each other.

Woke up this morning with a smile on my face, jumped out of bed, took a shower, dressed, cleaned up my place...

By the time the driver reached her house, Melissa woke up and felt as if she had downed a whole bottle of Tequila with no salt or lemon. Her mouth felt furry, as if she had just woken up from a hibernating sleep, but she knew it was just the result of good loving.

Taking one last look at the sexy interior, Melissa wobbled on her feet. Fresh air hit her and she sucked it in gladly.

She put one hand on her stomach, as if to gain some equilibrium and decorum. She felt that her night was painted, scene-by-scene, across her forehead.

When she got to her door, with Miles supporting her, he handed her a birthday card, which had an thick bulge inside it. She tilted her head to the side and smiled sweetly.
Hugging him tightly, Melissa whispered in his ear.

"Thank you for a beautiful birthday present. I'm gonna remember this for a while."

"No you won't, your gonna remember this forever," Miles smiled.

"Am I now?!"

"Damn right. Anyway, I gotta go home, this limo turns into a pumpkin in fifteen minutes. Get some rest and I'll call you tomorrow, 'cuz I have your number now."

"Make sure you do! Good night sweetheart."

A long, lingering kiss finalised their night and Miles walked down her path, closed her gate and waved at her through the open window as the limo pulled away.

Melissa watched the limo turn the corner and into the chasm of the early morning. She put her key in the lock, feeling the card and the strange bulge inside it.

What the hell could this be, she thought to herself as she closed the door quietly.

Shuffling to her bed, managing to take off her dress with one swoop, she put on her side lamp and collapsed on the bed with the card.

Melissa made short work of the envelope and looked at an all-black card with her name on the front in silver letters.

She lay on her stomach, with her feet dangling excitedly behind her.

She opened the card and saw a DVD with the words 'Smile your on camera' written on the front.

The smile on Melissa's face wasn't as big as her look of shock when she fumbled for the remote and put it on.

Miles and Melissa lit up the screen as they sat down and looked around the limousine earlier on.

Melissa turned off her side light and snuggled deep under her duvet as Miles began to tell her story over their limo footage.

She would thank Miles the next time she saw him.
Oh, would she thank him.

A heavy hand slapped Melissa across her face and woke her from the amazingly-detailed dream that made her thighs slippery, nipples rock hard and body hot as if summer crept under her sheets.
Her eyes slowly focussed on the ceiling; the swirling fan mesmerising her thoughts of Miles and how real he felt inside her.

A FUCKING DREAM, Melissa thought to herself. The limousine, the club, my legs in the air, my first blowjob, face down ass up, how the fuck was that a dream?

Running one hand over her sweaty face and the other between her thighs, Melissa tried to roll over but she slapped straight into Kelvin's hairy back. He replied by groaning heavily then rolling back onto her, his weight and morning breath pressing down on her.
His scent was warm; mixed with weed and Jägermeister as his lips pressed against her cheek.

Like an octopus, Kelvin's arms were everywhere and, after just having had Miles in her mind, Melissa felt repulsed by his touch.

His long fingers and even longer finger nails attempted a smooth caress up and down her thighs but, to her, it felt like Freddy Kruger was paying her a visit.
Moaning rhythmically, Kelvin began his regular trail down her body that, Melissa knew, would end with his fingers inside her and she was NOT in the mood for him.

Not now.

Miles' tongue was still doing that thing to her G-spot in her mind while Kelvin often mistook the curve of her labia minora for her clitoris. And when he eventually found it, his clit massage technique resembled someone trying to get a stubborn stain out of a shirt.

OH HELL NO...

"Babe," Melissa said sleepily.

"Come babe, I'm feeling it right now." Was Kelvin's reply. "You was supposed to give me some last night..."

"Yeah, and you fell asleep 'cuz you thought Jägermeister could be drunk out the bottle..."

Kelvin stepped up his efforts by grinding his small-to-medium erection against her back and assaulting her sensitive left breast with his Kruger claws.

"Babe, I can't..." Melissa said, unwrapping his tentacles from around her heated body.

"What'd you mean you can't? Why can't..."

"I came on my period last night after you fell asleep. So you missed out, sorry. Anyway, good night."

And with her lie delivered without a pause, Melissa rolled onto her side and sighed, giving Kelvin her back to stare at.
Behind her, she could hear him huffing and puffing, beating his pillows and dragging the covers away from her.

She didn't mind.

She was hot anyway.

Escaping Temptation

Stefan

A chocolate man, standing at a solid six foot three, was elbow deep in wires and cables under a makeshift desk, which was really an old door. He attempted to wrap them neatly in his space as he scanned the five security screens he set up in his cubby hole. One camera on the front door, one on the back door, two on the meeting spot and one dark screen.
He planned to arrive more than two hours before the meeting to set-up his cameras but today was not going according to plan. But it wasn't his fault... the spanner in his machine wasn't a what... but a who.
And this was not how he worked.

Well known in the criminal underworld of London town, Stefan was not only imposing as an enforcer but he excelled when it came to surveillance and plotting routes of escape out of tight situations. It was what he did. That was what the boss hired him for.
Any job he put his name on went like clockwork and he was proud of this perfect record that many gangsters could not obtain.
Because they were gangsters! Or at least tried to be. And gangsters were stupid as they were always blinded by their greed and need for acceptance and expansion, which always fucked them up in the end.

But it wasn't his fault that he was late, thus not able to set up all the microphones he wanted to plant in the bar, nor the thermal imaging monitor, which was always standard. This meant that anyone could walk in with a neatly hidden weapon that could fuck up EVERYTHING!
And by everything, Stefan wasn't thinking about the deal that was set to go down in Birds Of Paradise Bar, his mind was elsewhere.

Scanning the four working screens in front of him, happy with the space he'd created in his hole, Stefan sat back and exhaled. He stared at the ceiling and wondered if he was doing the right thing.
"You know, when you exhale, you sound like you're eating a piece of fruit that is sweeter than you thought it would be."

Her voice.
In his head.
Rattling around like a pinball, knocking against his wants, bashing against his baser animal instincts, slamming along his rationale.

Not good for business, he thought as her words made his stomach tingle.

He stared at each screen, watching for players in the game to appear but he had another 15 minutes before he EXPECTED anyone to arrive. Thinking like the criminals he worked for, he knew the OTHER SIDE would send their own 'computer whiz' to get to the venue early and scan it over for any potential danger issues. But Stefan was smoother than that and found the perfect spot to set up; an old cloak room with a door that looked like a part of the bar's exterior walls.
Their 'whiz' would never find it.

He ran a strong hand over his head, fiddled with the tracking on one of the camera screens and tried to ignore the voice that was still dancing in his subconscious.
Stefan wanted more than anything to allow the voice to two-step with his thoughts but he, of all people, knew how fucked up his professional life would become if he let his guard down.
That didn't make it any harder for Koko, the boss's girlfriend, to sell him a dream of leaving his life of working for others behind and make a new life with her.

Bang on her sales pitch which managed to connect with the lack of enjoyment he was feeling about his position in life.
Not that he wasn't happy... the amount of money he was making, there was no way he couldn't at least raise a smile. But, personally, he wasn't happy to make that money working with the type of people he did.
But leave it all?

His Pharrell Williams Dim The Lights ringtone sounded softly and he shook his train of thought and looked at the screen.
A question mark was ringing him.
He knew who it was without flinching, though he stared at the screen before answering.
Stefan sighed. "You can't keep calling me you know?"
"Why, scared I'll say something you like?"
"You already have."

"Well before we start singing Midnight Train To Georgia, you need to make sure your shit is ready 'cuz we're leaving now. Is EVERYTHING ready?"

Everything. EVERYTHING.

If Koko meant had he packed his life away into one duffel bag and stored it, then yes, he had everything ready.

"I've BEEN ready..."

"We'll see..." Koko whispered.

Stefan could hear HIS voice in the background before she hung up.

He was ready!

So ready that he flicked through his BlackBerry and watched the video he made while Koko gave him what can only be described as 'heavenly' head.

And in the boss's bed.

Koko

Sitting in the back of the limo, Koko sat nervously thinking over the plan.

Walter and his briefcase plopped beside her. He snorted phlegm down his throat and immediately opened the locket around his neck. He scooped angel dust with his baby finger nail, drawing the stardust up his huge nostril.

The same again with the other nostril.

Scoop, fly.

He rubbed the remaining residue on his gums.

"Hey baby, loosen up," Walter said, tipping some onto the corner of his credit card.

She put her tiny nostril to the card, with Walter watching her through glazed eyes as the dust vanished.

She took a long pull on her cigarette, flicking the ash out the window as they pull off.

Answering his phone with one hand, Walter slid his other hand between her legs, slipping his fingers up to her pussy.

Up close and personal, he kissed her neck and she tensed up.

"Stop please stop, STOP IT!" she shouts pushing him away.

Pissed at the rejection, he raised his fist, lining it with her jaw line without breaking his conversation. She flinches, lifting her hand to protect her face.

"I'd smack your face off if you didn't cost me so much with the brothers," he said running his tongue up the side of her face. "You know your my best skeezer, that's why your mine."

He forced his hand inside her crotch; caressing the walls of her love but she said nothing just silent tears rolling down her face. She chanted in her head:

"Just two more hours, just two more hours, just two more hours..."

Thirty minutes later, Koko strolled into the temple of fornication, lust and desires with Walter leading her way. Before they properly entered the busy bar, people approached Walter in respect of his arrival.

"Wah gwan bless, you cool?" Was Walter's chant for the first ten minutes.

A lady with skin the shade of honey and the figure of an hourglass greeted them.

"Good evening Walter."

"What's hanging Rachel?" he said, handing her his tailor-made coat.

"I'm sure you'll show me later."

Koko shoves her coat into the hostess hand thinking to herself, 'Fucking tart! The bitch doesn't even hide the fact she fucked Walter in MY bathtub today.'

"Get us two bottles of Cristal," Koko demanded.

"You best believe I'll show you what's hanging," Walter taunted, slapping Rachel on her apple bottom.

Koko walked off to the VIP seating area with Curtis Mayfield's Pusherman putting a swing in her step. There was something powerful about being a top gangster's girlfriend; it was a far cry from being pushed about when she was a nobody stripping for a tenner in Soho.

Placing her well-toned back spring on the cushy sofa, she watched people getting in the mood; flirting, touching, drinking, negotiating, snorting, drug taking and other recommended potions in motion. Weed smoke clung to the air like fog on a field but Koko's attention was on the cameras.

She caught a glimpse of a camera neatly tucked away in the corner of the bar. She kissed her index finger and blew a kiss to the camera, knowing Stefan was watching.

After a few minutes, four gentlemen walked in tandem to their

table. Eric, Ryan, Trevor and Dizzy, the other side's 'computer whiz'.
Koko greeted them all with half nods before excusing herself as she always does when Walter is doing business.

That was always the time to go 'powder' her nose.

She sauntered past dancing patrons on her way to the toilet, when she walked past an open door. Sniffing hard, she could see a room with men and women crowded in a circle, paying attention to something in front of them and sex in the air.
"Excuse me gentlemen," she said to a group of tall men watching.

They looked her up and down with hunger painted across their faces.
They parted like the Red Sea and she stepped between them. She could see them fighting the urge to touch her but she could see the respect in their demeanour.

They knew she was untouchable.

Etching her way to the front of the group, a waitress placed a flute of champagne in her well-manicured fingers.

Three women were on the floor before her; a thick woman with short, cropped hair and caramel skin was wearing a strap-on and had a second woman's legs wrapped round her body riding it like a tide. Koko couldn't make out the rest of her face because a third woman was sitting on it bouncing her ass on her waiting tongue, moaning tunes to a rhythm with the lyrics screaming, 'I'm about to cum'.

Koko was mesmerised.

Watching such freedom in front of her very eyes made her think of the freedom she would soon share with Stefan.

Searching for a camera, she took in the room and realised a ritual had begun. Men and women and women and women were touching each other, caressing, kissing, wanking and fucking. The ones that weren't doing anything were watching in amazement, there was something sexy about watching people fuck without a thought or care who was watching. And that was what kept Koko in place.

The performance turned her on so much, she could feel her panties starting to soak and cool against her warmth.
Satisfied with the eye-gasm, and planning to return, she took off towards the women's toilet, still enjoying the looks she wasn't

getting and the reasons why. She stopped in front of the toilet door to finish her drink and smooth down her Gucci dress when a hand snatched her from a hole in the wall into what looked like an old cloakroom.
"So THIS is where you been hiding, eh?"
She looked Stefan up and down like a massive piece of chocolate, licking her lips. Her breathing became heavy as she took in every inch of her 'sex god'.

Stefan

"I got the kiss you sent me," he said, feeling Koko's breath suck out of her as she nestled between his arms.
"I knew you were watching."
Koko's smile was Stefan's weakness as she kissed him with electricity and energy surging between them. He could feel her nervousness at being mere feet away from a man who would kill her if he could see through walls. And Stefan knew he'd be taking an earth nap on a building site somewhere in the foundations of the Olympic Village if this didn't go to plan.
Koko managed to jump into his grasp and wrap her thighs behind him, their kiss unbroken. Her body was excited to be around him and his erection told her the feeling was reciprocal.
With Koko attached to his lips, Stefan tried to talk, "Listen babe... we need to do this just right, otherwise, we're ALL fucked, ya understand?"

Unhitching her from his torso like a Velcro vixen, Stefan held her against his station of active monitors and looked into her eyes.
"Koko, I'm serious. You know what he's like when it comes to things like his DVDs so what do you think is gonna happen when he pieces this together?"
Fighting against his strong grip, Koko's heart was beating and she wriggled loose, allowing her hands to run up and down his, always warm, body.
"You think I care? Fuck him, fuck Eric, fuck Ryan, DEFINATELY fuck Trevor, ugly piece of shit. And fuck Dizzy... cock-eyed fucker! I don't care about anything else right now except for what's in this room... do you know what I just saw right outside..."
"KOKO? This is serious... this ain't no joke suttin', this is our lives here. We both know how trigger happy Trevor is... he wouldn't blink before shooting us both."
"Does that turn you on? The fact that you could die?" Koko

asked, her hands playing with his zip.
"Death doesn't REALLY do it for me you know. I'm more a fan of breathing normally, a big booty and living healthily."
Koko was lost in her fingers working his zip without him noticing. Her hand was trailing the inside of his trousers before he could react and she released his semi.
Her face was made up with deviousness; sneaky shadowing her eyes and cunning making her lips shine in his cubby hole.
If time wasn't so tight, Stefan would easily allow Koko to engage him. Use her hand to start working the length of his shaft, using his sticky pre-cum to slide more easily. Take him out of his trousers and drop to her knees in front of him.

With Walter sipping a Stella while feeling Rachel's available backside on his third monitor, Stefan looked down to see Koko folding him into her mouth.
"Koko, no... we don't have..."
Stefan knew it was too late. Lost in the thoughts of what she could be doing, he wasn't watching what she was actually doing and she caught him slipping. So she slipped him in.
Her lips pursed in front of his head, she slid him in slowly, pushing him through her closed mouth. She stopped mid-shaft and looked up at Stefan, who always loved to watch. Their eyes spoke as Walter huddled with his boys and cock-eyed Dizzy disappeared out of frame. Stefan wanted to follow him across the screens but Koko demanded his attention.

Her eyes and lips were soft and Stefan was a picture of control, but her eyes always did something to him. Soft, honey brown and asking him a question.

'Can I have it all?'

His deep, brandy brown eyes wanted to answer but time was not their friend and he could feel 'beef' rising in the air. But, with Koko, he felt like time could wait.

'You can have anything you want.'

Koko slipped her handbag off her shoulder, released her mouth, opened wide and took Stefan until her lips reached his stomach. She held her mouth open, flexing her throat against his length, saliva creating a slapping sound.
"Anything you want..." Stefan said, closing his eyes to the images

of the club that beamed behind Koko's kneeling frame.
She hummed on his dick and watched him react with a giggle, a sound that always made her feel good inside.
In the background, Stefan's black monitor came to life. The sudden change in light made him open his eyes, dragging himself from the ecstasy of Koko's warm mouth.
Reaching over to adjust the zoom, he saw a group of half naked people surrounding a...
"What the hell is this?" Stefan said, his body trembling from good head but his mind clouded with fear.
His escape room... the way out of this whole thing... his ace in the hole, was now compromised and he had no idea who the people were or where they came from. He just knew that his whole plan was fucked.
He raised the volume on the camera in the room and he could decipher three separate moans coming from the room. But he couldn't see what everyone was looking at.
Sliding his dick into her cheek, Koko turned to the screen and moaned. "That's the room I was trying to tell you about. There's some SHIT going on in there. Actually, leave the volume up."
Stefan didn't know what to say. He didn't know how to tell Koko that his big plan was fucked by the fact that people were... fucking.
His brow was now drenched and his heart was beating so fast, he could feel it in his throat. He had no time to think as Koko made his dick a sloppy mess in her grasp.
Watching her work, the way she slid saliva onto his dick and sucked it back into her mouth, was ALWAYS a mistake, but he always looked.
"Baby... look... oh shiiiiiiit.... babe... I've gotta... gotta..."
    Stefan stopped speaking as his hips spoke for him and thrust his wet dick into Koko's open mouth, with her tongue out. He held her head steady and circled his hips.
Walter's sudden movement on the monitor drew his attention. His boss was now drawing a weapon and running out of the camera's sight.
"Oh shit... babe..."
Stefan looked down again and met Koko's dreamy brown eyes and felt his body warming up and a cold shiver running down his back.
Gunshots rang out in the club and Stefan's camera screens were a scurry of activity, people running towards exits, random shooters

popping off and Walter disappearing and reappearing on every screen.
His last movements were caught on one screen and Walter had his gun cocked, walking in their general direction.
Koko didn't flinch. "You better come in my mouth."

Koko

Koko realised she was losing Stefan's attention to the commotion that was going on behind her on the monitors. She heard three loud shots which startled her, almost making her jam her teeth into the flesh between her lips.
Stefan snatched his piece from her mouth; he was concentrating on the screens before him. Koko watched his dick dry before her eyes.
She stood up, turned his face to hers and kissed him passionately, forcing her tongue in his mouth.
One kiss was all it took to make him forget about Walter running around Bird's Of Paradise Bar with his favourite gun out, ready to shoot anyone who stood in his way.

Koko's heart beat for Stefan, for the two of them.
They shared a forbidden love they tried so hard to avoid, for they toyed with death. But in the end it didn't stop Stefan pulling Koko into his strong arms, sharing deep passionate kisses.
His finger's wandered into Koko's knickers and, with the madness going on in the bar drifting away, brought back memories of when she first met him.

    She was lying in the sun on a lounger by the pool reading a book, his delicious cologne arrived before he did. She looked up to see a delectable specimen of a man standing before her. The fire in her belly was instant.
    She would daydream about him doing the same thing; putting a fire in her belly. Just to put his hands in her knickers and play with her, to have those long fingers caress her walls when Walter was drunk by the pool. He always managed to bring back the same feelings of lust that made her weak every time, there was no one who would tell her otherwise.
All those times when Stefan would come to 'check up' on her when Walter was away on business trips were spent exploring the heights of sexual creativity in his eight-bedroom mansion in

Hertfordshire.

In Koko's mind, body and soul, they had a future to be erected, but first they had a past to escape.

Koko's hands wandered back to Stefan's piece, not once taking any notice of the gunshots ringing around her. In his presence she felt safe and knew that he had a plan to get them out of there. She played with his sticky pre-cum and welcomed his hardness, his fingers inside her walls and his tongue on her teeth.
Pulling his buttons off his tailored shirt, she ran her hands under his vest and over his corrugated stomach.
He unzipped her dress peeling her out like a banana; revealing her plump breasts and beautiful skin, watching it drop to the floor. Koko sighed at his charisma, his talent to make her forget to breathe.
He pulled her lace panties down, careful not to tangle them in her heels.
She stood in front of him like a perfect painting.
Glistening beads of sweat ran down her back in the dimly lit furnace of a cloak room. Wearing nothing but Prada heels and a diamond choker, to cover the bruises Walter put around her neck, Koko stepped into Stefan's breathing space. He picked her up with ease and placed her on the desk, parting her legs wide and high.

Staring into her eyes, he dropped to one knee in front of her pursed her lips with his tongue, the sensation making her hold her breath.

She felt his warm wet tongue dive in to her opening.

Letting out a moan, she pushed her hips into his chin, holding his head as she fucked his tongue.
Stefan knew how to heal her from the inside and make all her anxieties go away, calming her instantly.

Grinding her hips frantically, her moans ringing in his ears, the gun shots popping in the distance, all combined but didn't faze either of them.
Her moans told him she was going to burst her juices on his face but he kept sucking her swollen clit, her favourite sensation. She played with her nipples sucking them; encircling her tongue on the left one, the right one, both.
Her pussy contracted, letting a warm liquid coat Stefan's mouth. The show made his dick harder.

He stood up while licking his lips, pulled her toward him and kissed her, letting the essence of her smother their kiss.
Koko pushed him back until he hit the chair with his leg. He was forced into the seat before he could make the decision and she straddled him, with perfect aim. Letting him into her wetness, she began to ride him, waiting for him to throw his head back as he always did.
Gunshots still popping off, deafening screams, but it was Koko and Stefan's world.
Koko kept riding him, sending him into a trance. The sensation oh so good, so good.
He stood up making her stand with him and turned her round, making her touch the ground.
A rude intrusion but mind blowing sensation inside her pussy and goosebumps frazzled her body, sending her into outer space with her mind in another dimension.

    He stroked her, stirred her coffee. She tried to stand, but he forced her head down to her knees, bringing her perfect peach into his dick while his balls beat against clit. He found his favourite spot inside her and made himself at home.
Koko bit her bottom lip, she could almost taste the blood filling its plump pinkness.

Stefan

    With no warning, three loud shots popped off and Stefan looked at the screens to see Walter kicking and bussing shots at the door to their cubby hole.

Koko was completely bent over and couldn't see what the silent screen was showing but he could hear the impact of the bullets sucking into the wall of bulletproof vests he attached to the door upon his arrival.
Without panicking, Stefan moved quickly. He knew the door wouldn't hold for long but long enough to get done what he needed to do.
Koko began to alternate the flick of her cheeks, making sure he was as deep as he could go. Holding onto her ankles, Koko pounded on his dick, while he tried to reach into the pocket of his trousers which were bunched around his ankles. Koko was pounding him, using the table above her to catch herself and rock backwards and forwards into him.

Pressing a small pen in his pocket, two panels from the ceiling separated and two thick wires dropped to the floor.

Frantically, Stefan tried to focus away from Koko's apple shape and the moistness that was dripping off his testicles and hook her up. Attempting to attach one of the wires around Koko's moving waist, Stefan kept an eye on the door of vests, which was wobbling.

"Kinky time now?" Koko asked from below.

With his dick hard, wet and getting wetter, Stefan attached Koko's wire around her waist securely then hooked his.
"OPEN THE FUCKING DOOR... I KNOW YOU'RE IN THERE... MY GUN KNOWS YOU'RE IN THERE WITH MY BITCH..."
"Is that Walter?" Koko said, trying to stand upright.
"Shhh..." Stefan returned, drawing his trousers up, but leaving his zip down. He slung his rucksack over his back and took ONE safety check on everything before he turned off the lights. Working the controls in the dark, with Koko's sugar walls flexing, he zoomed in on the screen showing Walter at a medium close up.

"Hey Walter?" Stefan said, watching his boss react to his voice.
"You know you're a fucking dead man don't you? You DO know that?"
"I'd rather live with this..."

And with that, Stefan held Koko's waist tight and slowly worked his dick in and out of her until she built up to a steady moan that he knew Walter would hear. He bent his legs so he entered from below while spreading her cheeks with one hand and spanking her with the other.

"Stef... an... who... whoo... whooo..."

Koko was now leaning on the table, grinding on him in the dark while Walter continued to lick shots at the door.
Reaching under her body, Stefan used two fingers to letterbox her clit and she shuddered instantly, letting out a guttural moan that built to the tip of her voice.
"Now that, BOSS, is how you make YOUR woman come."

Stefan knew that would more than infuriate Walter and his action promoted his boss's reaction as he disappeared from the screen and reappeared holding an AR-15 assault weapon at the door.
But more importantly than the military-issued assault rifle he was

holding was the fact that, for the first time today, Walter wasn't holding his precious briefcase.
Exactly what Stefan hoped for.
"SHIT," Stefan said as he reached for this pocket again. "Hold on baby... hold that position."

Wrapping his arms around Koko's vibrating waist, and thrusting himself deep enough to stay inside her, Stefan clicked the tip of the pen. The wires suddenly retracted and slowly pulled them off the ground and through the open panels and into a pitch black vent.
Koko, who viewed the whole thing while holding her ankles, watched the ceiling panels close behind them as they jerked to a sudden stop.

Silence.
New darkness.

Koko could feel her legs dangling but couldn't see them in the black before her eyes. The vent was musty and she could hear the scuttling of feet all around her. But Stefan's strong arm around her waist told her she was fine.
She felt for a steady surface to walk her hands up in order to hang upright.
"What the fuck just..."
"Shh... watch this..."
Stefan showed Koko a night-vision video feed of the room they just disappeared from. On the screen, the door burst open and Walter, gun in one hand and briefcase in the other, stumbled into the dark room with his weapon trained on everything.
Walter felt a path with his legs, intent on not getting caught slipping by one of the best tricksters in the gangster game.
Anything he knocked into came face-to-face with the muzzle of the rifle and Stefan enjoyed watching him stumble in the darkness. All his gangster power, his strength, his command of life and death, stripped away and left a small boy with a big gun stumbling in the dark.
Above him, Stefan counted down in his head from 60, while Koko turned to face him, awakening his dangling dick with her moist grip.
Building a slow rhythm, with the swing of the wires, Stefan wrapped Koko's legs around his waist. As easy as his erection

slipped into her, it felt like he was meant to be there.

"48... 47... 46... 45...44..." Stefan counted, using the light from the video screen to illuminate Koko's face.

"Why you counting?"

"...42... You'll see... 40..."

"So I've got time to do this then?"

Koko wrapped her arms around his shoulders and lifted herself up and down on him. He was submerged in her pillow soft insides and with her Gucci dress bunched around her waist, she used her exposed pussy as a lubricant and worked around the wires that suspended them.

Stefan closed his eyes as Walter prowled in the darkness, using his gun to feel out the room. Stumbling on a chair, Stefan figured out where Walter was in the room.

Koko was now holding his mini-LED screen so he could see the room and used the light to shine on his face as he struggled to count.

"...33...32...3...1..."

"By the time you get to 15, I'm gonna come..."

With their eyes locked, and Walter stumbling below, Koko exhaled as Stefan inhaled, riding against the sway of their bodies.

Her feet stretched behind him and found the back of the vent, giving her some leverage.

They didn't share any kisses, they just stared at each other, their faces daring the other to flinch.

"... 26... 25... 5... 24... 23... 3... 3... oh 3..."

Koko was thumping her hips on his dick and her circular movement took his focus momentarily. And in all his years doing what he did, this was a first.

Stefan grinned. "... 22... 21...20..."

"Keep counting baby..." Koko whispered.

CRASH...

Stefan kept his eyes firmly on Koko, watching her lips fight to stay closed and not let out the scream she was dying to release. He didn't care what Walter crashed into underneath because, in a few more seconds, it was all going to be over.

"... 19... 18..."

Her hand popping his erection in and out of her quickly was the right note for her song as Stefan watched her struggle to stay silent.

"Shhh... 17... 16..."

"I... I can't... can't... oh... oh... ohhh... STEF..."

Stefan froze. "Oh shit..."

As she built to her crescendo, Stefan immediately looked at the screen expecting the worst. And the worst is what stared back at him.

Walter was looking up at the panels above him and was in the process of swinging the gun towards the ceiling, in their direction, while Koko was bucking against him.

"...FAN ... I'm coming..." she finished shouting.

"Shit... Hold on..."

Wrapping his arms around her again, Stefan released the pulley system with the click of the pen and the pair of them fell straight through the ceiling panels, bringing four surrounding panels crashing down with them.

With a whole heap of noise, Stefan broke through first with his feet and was able to kick the barrel of the gun away from their direction as they dropped.

Stefan's other foot landed a crunching kick in Walter's face and, though it happened so quickly, he was sure he heard and felt something crack.

Trying to stick the landing, while holding Koko was harder than Stefan thought and he managed to semi-land on his feet. He slipped on the cables he fought so hard to put away earlier and fell backwards with Koko on top of him onto the crumpled Walter, who was motionless beneath them.

Stefan twisted his ankle on the way down and knew it was more than a sprain, but he knew his feet were the least of his worries. Least he managed to score two good kicks.

Koko was sucking air through her teeth as she let out a low moan that sounded like pleasure and pain.

"You ok? You should be, you landed on me."

"Wasn't that the plan?" Koko replied.

"Not really..."

Stefan hobbled up and pulled Koko to her feet before she was ready. She swayed on her feet, expecting her stilettos to help support her but her heels were lost in the madness.

"Looking for these?"

While wrestling the briefcase from Walter's quiet carcass, Stefan drew Koko's attention to her heels which were embedded in his ex-boss's temple. His bloody face was slumped to the side and yet he still managed to sport that 'fuck you' grin.

"Is he..."

"Do you wanna find out or do you wanna get out of here and fly?" Stefan asked, dusting her down and straightening her diamond choker.
"Let's fly... fly every time..."

Stefan looked back at the fallen, possibly deceased, Walter. As he held Koko in his arms and manoeuvred them between the hole they made, he smiled.
"Ready baby?"

Looking down at Walter, who was literally wearing her heels with a smile, brought a sense of relief over Koko as she looked back to Stefan.
　　She spat on the quiet Walter and sighed heavily.
"I had the best orgasm you know," she said, running her hands over his face.
"Sorry I missed it... maybe we can take the wires with us and try again somewhere else," Stefan replied and pressed the button in his pocket.

　　Quicker than before, the pair of them were sucked back into the vent by their waists and up towards the roof, where Stefan had his cousin Royston, who was a full-fledged helicopter pilot, on standby.
The sound of the air passing by them made them feel like they were flying. Koko hugged him and held onto his body as tight as she could.
　　They did not plan to let each other go.

Passion Play

Pashun Nate

This is my ode to big dick
My pussy request for something nice and thick
To rub against my clit

Pass Ion

I heard your ode and this is dick
Your pussy will surely fit my thick

Push me on the bed
And fuck me quick

What you waiting for
I got this stick
Right here for you to sit

Handcuff my hands
Because I love that freaky shit

Now you're on the bed
One arm, one leg are cuffed as I fuck you in the bed

Spank me hard
When you ride me with that magic stick

I dig you deep,
I dick you quick
And I ride you with the magic stick

Give me that
Creamy cum to lick

Nah, nah I'm not ready to come
Be patient, let me get my tongue

Wide legged
On a chair I sit

Flick and stick you
For your turn to come

Hit me from the back
Cos I'm your nasty chick...

That makes me want to
devour it

Do Me Right

Pulling into Hoe road, Cassandra was glad the weekend was finally here.

Working like a slave in a sweaty press office, hearing her name screamed from every corner – or a shortened variation – rushing around like a blue ass fly answering calls; it was too much for her Nubian frame.

She regularly took time out from her day by walking around in the empty renovated floors above her office to NOT kill someone. Those strolls helped keep her queen etiquette about her statuesque figure and were perfect in the winter when she refused to smoke outside.

Blessed with a full, phat shape, Cassandra caught the looks as she past desks and entered offices. But she didn't mind; she knew she was sculpted with a firm pair of breasts (no droop), flat, with a minuscule pudge, stomach and her own basketball-shaped behind. Everything else fell into perfect chocolate place.

Leon knew it too... he spent enough time pounding that same behind during hours of foul mouthed, sheet staining sex that left her breathless until sleep slapped in.

Lover of mystery and one big nerve ending, Leon was an enigma, stuck in a conundrum, wrapped in secrecy, covered in confusion and they had been making the bed bang for over eight months and, somehow, he made every time feel like the first time.

Not too soft from behind, not too hard when her legs were on his shoulders and just the right amount of force in the leg scissors, Leon was a good meal.

So much was she falling into him that Cassandra was thinking of letting him into the inner sanctum of trust that she held around her queen-dom.

Thinking, of course.

One of the strikes against him was that she did not know a lot about him. Sure she knew his dick felt like it came up to her throat when he fucked her and he had the restraint of a saint when she unleashed her Super Sayian head game but where were his parents from, what was his favourite meal, how did he learn not to come for so long?

What she did know about him was that he was a stunning specimen of chocolate black man; pencil-thin dreadlocks down to his shoulders, always smelled like honey and man, muscular arms and not afraid to go down without question or head pushing.

As she pulled up to her Enfield abode, Cassandra took her key out of the ignition and let her head rest.

"Finally home," she said, exhaling.

Beads of sweat slipped between her cleavage, tickling her chest as she picked her shopping bags and weekend work off the back seat, shuffling tiredly to her front door.

Searching her holdall-sized handbag, through mountains of bills, tissues, notes and chewing gum, she found her keys and looked up, almost jumping out of her skin.

"My queen," Leon said, appearing out of nowhere. "Hard day at work?"

"Fucking hell, you scared the shit out of me. Where did you come from?" Cassandra replied, planting a shaky kiss on his lips.

"Been here the whole time. Watched you sit in the car, taking a little moment... that was cute."

"That was stress mate. Just glad the weekend's here," Cassandra exhaled, slipping her key into the door.

Before she pushed it open, she backed into Leon and felt what she thought she saw when he first materialised.

His erection.

That strong, unfaltering rod that was her own personal vibrator. Never ran out of batteries, was there whenever she needed it and came attached with an absolutely gorgeous black man, as standard.

"Think you're gonna get some do ya?" she said, grabbing his groin behind her.

Leon whispered, "The mere fact you've even asked me that question tells me you're at least THINKING about giving me some."

Taking her by surprise, Leon swept her off her feet – handbag, shopping bags, files and all – and took her in his arms over the threshold of her flat. Weaving her through the corridor, missing her head on doorways and carvings on the wall, Leon nudged the living room door open.

He placed her on the sofa, his strong arms flexing by her head.

"That's what I call door-to-door serv..."

"Shhh..." Leon silenced her with a finger on her lips.

Maybe it was the fact that it was the weekend or that her

vibrator was here and looked good enough to eat in a simple t-shirt and tracksuit bottoms but Cassandra felt the stress of work start to ooze away.

Dropping her bags to the floor, she felt her feet kick out in anticipation of whatever he was going to do next.

And with Leon, she never knew.

Foot massages, vertical 69s up against a wall, regular rimming, Leon made sure Cassandra was well catered for.

He carried an air that spread whenever she was around him. He brought out this animal in her that she wasn't fully aware of nor did she understand. Whenever Leon held her in his arms, she wanted to hold him so tight, her nails could pierce his skin.

And any time he had her thighs in his grip, her London voice took on a Jamaican drawl that disappeared with her following orgasm.

The Jamaican lady ALWAYS made an appearance pre-orgasm.

For Cassandra, this type of loving made her growl like a dog but she couldn't control the sound because she had no idea where it came from.

Her body would feel him and her voice box would respond.
But this just made her hungry for him... all the time.
Hungry for that fine plate of mysterious food.

Dropping to one knee in front of her, he traced his finger slowly from her lips where he shushed her. He trailed down her chin, through the middle of her cleavage, down her stomach, tickling her left thigh and down to her feet.

Gently and never taking his eyes off her, Leon slipped her shoes off and flexed her toes through her tights. Back and forth he flexed her tootsies, hearing and feeling them crack. Her head dropped back and she let out a sigh of contentment, feeling protected and looked after.

His soft touch on her feet was a guaranteed way to make her thighs moist and her mouth water. Leon's gentle fingers were the magic contact to the taps inside her and he always managed to make them flow.

His strong hands crept up her calf muscles and massaged. It was as if he knew where she needed to be touched, his fingers rolling a soft soul melody against her skin.

"Oh that's..." Cassandra whispered to herself.

"I know... that's the place innit?" Leon replied, concentrating and watching.

"Don't stop doing that..."

"First things first, are you hungry?" Leon asked.

"Hell yes, you best to feed me..." she followed, squirming in her seat.

"No, no, no, I mean are you hungry for food, like Chinese, pasta, I could do you a wicked..."

Cassandra chimed in, "...OR, I could just have you with a side of you, a tall glass of you on the side and for dessert, you covered in me."

"So no food?"

"All I need right now is..."

Her last word was a grab for his erection that was stretching against the crotch of his tracksuit bottoms. She got lost in a reminder to return the pant suit she bought last weekend.

It was the large hanger in the small plastic bag that connected her thoughts.

Leon stood up and smiled, watching Cassandra sway from side-to-side in a state of pleasure, squirming for him to touch her.

"Shall we take this to..."

Leon didn't finish his sentence because Cassandra awoke from her trance and sat straight up while, at the same time, yanking his tracksuit bottoms to the floor and controlling his erection with her lips.

She didn't need her hands; she was not adverse to putting Leon in her mouth using her lips. In fact she was quite skilled with her mouth and used her tongue and sometimes her teeth to get him off, with no effort. Leon's baritone moans told her she had the skills to use enough pressure from her teeth to make it feel good.

She licked the sides, making Leon's dick gleam. He knew she was preparing him for her deepthroat.

As per usual, Leon's head pointed straight to the ceiling as she took him deep into her mouth and hummed at his base. The vibrations tickled along her tongue and the underside of his dick and he couldn't even move.

Slipping back to his tip, Leon's dick was glimmering with saliva. Loose drops lined the length of him and Cassandra wasted no time in sucking it back and taking him easily into her throat, purposely gagging.

Leon could feel his resolve letting go as he...

"Okay, stop." He said breathlessly. "Allow me."

And with that, he scooped her up again and kissed her full and deep. His tongue probed the outline of her lips, making them wet. Nibbling on her lower lip, Leon felt Cassandra's body relax on the way to her bedroom, his legs imprisoned in his bunched tracksuit bottoms.

"Where we going?" Cassandra asked with a smile, her sultry voice proving effective on Leon's eager dick.

"Like you don't know." Leon replied, shuffling like a penguin.

Cassandra's bedroom lit up as she flicked the light switch on the way in.

Laying her down softly, Leon stood up straight and removed his t-shirt, revealing a strong torso, broad shoulders and drummer's arms.

Cassandra, as always, loved to watch Leon undress. The way his body moved and flexed with each item of clothing disappearing opened her taps a little bit more. The desire in his face at what was about to happen knocked the taps off and let her water flow free.

She wasted no time in removing her office skirt, shirt and French knickers, flicking them to the floor, unhooking her bra, de-strapping, pulling and sliding it through her fitted t-shirt.

Leon was naked first.

"Ready?" he asked standing over her.

She replied by reaching out for his dick, ready to slip him back into her eager mouth.

His retort was to move out of her reach, walk round to the foot of the bed and part her thighs.

"Close your eyes," Leon commanded.

Her mind, body and soul wanted to do whatever he told her to do but her stubbornness wanted to keep her eyes open in protest.

Staring at her with a frown, Leon delivered attitude. Whenever he told her what to do, she followed suit without fail or question.

His strong voice was an aphrodisiac and she had no control over herself when he spoke in his demanding tone.

It had the power to open her thighs, blow a cool breeze

across her nipples and make her fidget uncontrollably. Whatever he wanted, she would give to him, just as long as he spoke in that deep tone.

Her desire to growl was growing.

Taking in the sight of his muscular nakedness at her feet, with his hands on her thighs, Cassandra closed her eyes and allowed her remaining senses to keep her informed.

Touch told her that he was still at the base of the bed; standing over her, hearing said that he was now bending down as his knees hit the floor and her clit told her that she was under serious threat of an immediate orgasm.

Leon bent down and watched her pussy squirm under his feather-light touch. He could feel that she wanted him to touch her directly but Leon wanted to make her wait and, really, he liked to watch her squirm.

Trimmed to a low fade, Cassandra's pussy was willing and able and her thighs were wide and ready but Leon wanted to savour the moment.

Using his thumb, he brushed across her clit and followed with his tongue. Cassandra's back curved off the bed and fell back, as if she'd been hit with a spoonful of electricity. Her breathing was laboured and her eyes were struggling to stay closed.

"Do that... again..." she whispered.

So he did.

Leon stuck two fingers in his mouth, making them wet and dripping and slipped her clit between his moist fingers, exposing her button.

Cassandra sucked a huge amount of air through her teeth as her head rolled on her pillow.

"Ready?" Leon asked, sarcastically.
"Are you taking the piss?"

With her thighs at east and west, Leon stuck his tongue out and labouredly licked her exposed clitoris. Slow and concentrated, Leon made sure he slipped up and down her pussy lips, tasting her pre-sex juice, lapping at her opening.

Cassandra could feel the stress of the office slipping further away with each flick of his tongue.

"Lick it harder... make me black out like you do..."

That was all Leon needed to hear as he dived in, wrapping his lips around her entire vagina, slipping his tongue deep inside her and using his teeth to rub gently against her clit.

Cassandra's sense of hearing told her that Leon was making her pussy wet and sloppy, just the way she liked it and touch told her she better stop him otherwise she might...

"Oh... oh... oh no... not... yet... OH..."

Holding onto the back of Leon's head, trying to create distance between them, Cassandra could feel her orgasm washing over her like shower water. It started at the top of her scalp and was working its way down to the soles of her feet. With each flick of his tongue and the added friction of her clit against his teeth, Cassandra knew it was going to be a huge one.

And she didn't even put a towel down.

The more she tried to move pull his head away, the sweeter his mouth felt.

Flick... touch says yes, grind, touch says hell yes, rub, hearing says make it sound good, flick, orgasm says I'm on my way.

"You coming baby?" Leon asked with his mouth full.

"Shh..." Cassandra replied, her pussy replaced with Leon's face. The more she worked her pussy into his face, the deeper his tongue went and the more she wanted to grind.

"Don't stop... that... oh I'm gonna come..." Cassandra said breathlessly. "Oh I'm gonna come all over your face... all over... all... over... oh... here... I..."

Grind, hip roll, flick, grind, hip roll, insert...

Before she could speak again, Cassandra came heavily on Leon's face. Her orgasm was loud, tense and very very wet.

During her short, sharp scream, Leon would pause as she bucked against him then slip his tongue deep in her silence.

A regular trick used to prolong the orgasm and give her no breaks in between.

"Stop... that..." she stammered.

With a sheen on his chin, Leon sat up and looked at the satiated Cassandra, who was grinning though her eyes were still closed.

Growling a hungry sound in the back of her throat, Cassandra motioned for him to kiss her. While licking liquid from his lips, he stroked his way up her sizzling body and held his lips above her own, while rubbing his erection against her throbbing clit.

Sense of smell told her that he was directly above her face.

"You good?" he asked.

"Why... do you... ask silly questions? You see me struggling... to... breathe..."

Cassandra grabbed the back of his head again and kissed him hungrily. Their tongues crossed, their desire had them chewing on each other's lips, stroking each other's faces and humming with pleasure.

She held his face in front of hers and opened her eyes. She stared deep into his pupils and felt herself almost slipping away.

Those beautiful eyes. Curved sexily in the corners for maximum bedroom effect and the same mahogany brown of his skin tone.

Dangerous if she stared for too long. The type of eyes that made her do silly things like invite him to move in with her, buy him a car or offer to pay HIS bills.

She didn't do those things but he got her close to saying some outlandish things once or thrice.

With Leon's face in her hands, Cassandra's tongue stuck out and licked his chin, slowly circling his lips and cheeks.

The taste of herself was a love supreme. During a private rub down session, she would often suck her fingers after an orgasm and feel another one building almost instantly. But more than anything, she loved to taste herself off someone else. Maybe it was the shared knowledge of sipping from the same cup, but she always tasted better on Leon's face.

He closed his eyes and worked his hips, allowing his pre-cum to slip down his crown and onto Cassandra's clit.

The slippery electricity was insane as Leon circled his hips slowly.

He's on some serious hard wine, Cassandra thought.

Hard wine, rubbing down wallpaper, cribbing, whatever you call it, Cassandra could feel it. His strong dick made little circles on her clit and she could take no more.

Reaching for a condom and blindly strapping him up, she took his dick and lined it up with her opening. Holding each other's gaze, they both seemed to stop breathing as Leon held back from entering.

His head rested softly on the door of her pussy but didn't enter, slowly circling again.

Cassandra's moan told him she was more than ready and her eager hip movements agreed.

"No... not yet..." Leon said.

"What'd you mean not yet? What the fuck?" Cassandra replied, a hint of annoyance in her voice.

"Look... just cool... down..."

With his last word, Leon plunged himself deep into Cassandra until there was nowhere left for him to go.

With her back arched, her voice missing and balancing on her head, Cassandra couldn't move with the feeling of a building orgasm shaking her thighs.

Ignoring her rigidity, Leon withdrew and plunged himself deep inside her again.

She wrapped her arms around his back and her thighs around his bum and moaned.

Deep, thrust, yes, grind, deep, stay, don't move, yes, no, another one...

Her chest was visibly pumping and her skin was shaking from the power of her last orgasm.

"How are you doing this?" she asked, struggling to catch the breath that was eluding her.

"Just giving you what you need," Leon replied, looking deep into her eyes.

"Don't look at me with those eyes. I know what you're doing."

"What am I doing? I'm just..."

Thrust, deep, quick, withdraw, clit touch, rub, enter, slippery friction, deep, deep, so deep, G-spot deep...

Looking into his eyes as he pumped her pussy with vigour and definite power, Cassandra could feel her nipples hardening at the effort on his face. Biting his lower lip, Leon was working hard and Cassandra appreciated every stroke, every motion, every drip.

Burying his face in her shoulder, Leon's hips became a blur as he began to pump himself faster and faster inside her. In between each thrust, Cassandra tried to talk to him but he wasn't listening.

"Stop... stop... stop... it... no... way... not... fair... oh... yes... harder..."

"Keep telling me no," Leon whispered in her ear.

Thrust, slip, slide, deep, in, out, circular motion, grind, grind, GRIND...

"NO... OH... my... fucking... god!"

Cassandra's legs slid up to his back and she held on for dear life as she could feel another orgasm awakening inside her. At this rate, he was going to kill her with pleasure or dehydration. She was losing more liquid with each orgasm and Leon showed no signs of coming any time soon.

As per usual.

Opening her lips, Cassandra sighed.

"No... no... do you... hear me... I'm saying no..."

"No, yeah? You sure?"

Leon's grunting into her shoulder turned into kissing which turned into nibbling, which turned into biting.

With one hand on her thigh and the other wrapped in her hair, Leon dug deep inside her and stayed there, allowing her to grind out her own orgasm.

Round, grind, round, grind, deep, deeper, deeper...

Leon could hear her dripping out and onto his dick, which was swimming inside her.

"Should've put a towel down... you know how you get," Leon said.

Cassandra looked up at him through hazy eyes and frowned with her breath on sprinter speed.

"Yeah... thanks... for the... advice. If... if... if you weren't trying to... kill me, I would've thought of that."

"Sorry," Leon said, making small hip movements that had the desired effect.

"Oi? Stop moving! You think I can't feel that?"

"If you can feel that, then you can feel..."

"Don't you dare..." Cassandra said, pushing him away at the same time. "You MUST be trying to kill me with that pole you call a dick."

"Not kill, please."

Still on her back, Cassandra took a solitary moment to compose herself while Leon watched her equilibrium return slowly.

"Please huh? Okay then... if THAT'S the rule..."

With a quick burst of renewed vigour, Cassandra moved quick enough to catch Leon off guard. She rolled him, sat up, jumped off the bed, pushed him into her spot and jumped on top of him, with thin trails of liquid trickling down her inner thighs.

Taking him in hand between her thighs, she looked deep into his eyes. "Ready?" she asked.

"Don't try and use my lyrics 'cuz..."

Before he could finish, she slammed down on top of him and used her wetness to shut him up.

And it did.

Her walls were drip drip wet and her clit was inflated and more sensitive than ever.

Her nipples were rock hard and were begging to be touched, so she used her thumb and index finger to squeeze the pleasure out of them. But she just turned herself on even more.

Squeeze, roll, lick, pinch, pain, yes, ohhh, lick, pinch, oh yes...

Cassandra got lost in her own self-pleasure as Leon wrapped his hands around her waist and locked his fingers. Pumping in rhythm to her bouncing, Leon held her ass cheeks open, trying to get deeper inside.

"Don't go there... I'm... supposed to be... fucking yo... fucking... fucking hell... tah rass..."

She trailed off in a Jamaican accent and growled again through her sudden squirt explosion on top of him.

His groin, stomach and legs were drenched and he could feel a growing patch forming on the sheet beneath him.

Cassandra collapsed into his neck, huffing and puffing. But his house was still standing inside her.

Her skin was throbbing and was hotter than Encona pepper as she hummed to herself.

Breathing labouredly, Cassandra didn't move.

Breathe, breathe, breathe, breathe, tense up, don't move, hold on, oh, oh OH, breathe, breathe, breathe...

"You okay?" Leon asked from below.

Cassandra managed to get a sentence together. "Not yet... you... might have... broken something... in... there."

"Huh?"

"I... can't stop..."

Breathe, breathe, breathe, shake, tense, squeeze, move, little bit, tense, oh, oh, OH, OH, OH, breathe breath breathe...

"Were you going to say coming?"
"Yeah... that..."

Cassandra couldn't see his face but she could feel a smile rise on Leon's face. Though he had every right to smile, giving her orgasm after orgasm, Cassandra felt like she needed to give him such an orgasm that would equal the quivering mess that she was now.

But she still couldn't move.

She wanted to but any movement brought on another wave of goodness and she was trying to breathe through it. Plus Leon wasn't helping; slow grinding inside her.

"You're not helping you know," Cassandra said.
"No? Oh, sorry," he replied.

Closing her eyes and sucking in as much air as her lungs could take, Cassandra rolled off Leon's still standing dick and curled into a ball next to him. She planned to slide down his body and give him the best blowjob of his life. But her body told her something different and she couldn't help but listen.

"You okay baby?" Leon asked, concerned.

"YOU!?! You don't talk to me ever again. Unless you figure out how to turn off this thing that you've turned on, don't talk to me."

"Oh, so it's like that?" Leon replied, leaning on his side to watch his handiwork.

"I'm STILL shaking so yeah, it's like that."

"Okay, let me help then."

Leon wrapped his arms around her and pulled her back into his front, spooning her body perfectly. Beads of sweat dripped from him to her and vice versa as her body shook under his strong grasp. Though he tried to tighten his grip whenever she shook, he couldn't do anything to prevent the good feeling that continued to wash over her.

"How's this?" he asked, locking his fingers over her stomach.
"It's not better, I'm still coming…"
"I know, your whole body is shaking…"
"Well done, hope your proud of yourself."
"Should I be?"
"Are you asking stupid questions again?"

Breathe, breathe, breathe, shake, tense, squeeze, breathe, breathe, breathe… oh, oh, OH…

That was the last thing Cassandra remembered saying to Leon that evening.

She didn't recollect when she stopped shaking but she knew she was still in her bed.

And she was asleep.

Waking up suddenly, Cassandra looked around the room, fighting off disorientation.

It was night-time, street lights were blazing and she was lying on her side, still rolled up in a ball.

Reaching over, she found Leon's space empty and his touch missing.

"Leon?" she called out. "Leon?"

Rolling onto her back, she spread her arms out and stretched long and hard. She felt her legs, knees, arms, elbows, fingers and toes crack at the same time.

Stretching out her arm, she heard the crumple of paper on the bed next to her.

Fumbling in the dark, she turned on her bedside lamp and found a piece of paper with Leon's handwriting on it.

Still feeling the residual effects of her shake-a-thon, Cassandra exhaled and rubbed her eyes.

She started to read:

Dear Cass,
I came to see you today to tell you something but, when I saw you, it went right out of my head. But as you know, that's what you do to me. Unfortunately, I wasn't coming to give you good

news.

I'm leaving the country tonight. My band is going on tour of Australia and Asia and we have to leave on a flight to Malaysia. Tonight. I wanted to tell you face-to-face but seeing you, I couldn't help myself with you.

And, more importantly, you seemed to need... something. But maybe it's better this way. This way we won't have to act like a couple saying goodbyes and 'I'll call you' and 'I'll email you'.

I'll be back in six months or so but I'll always be thinking of you. How can I forget the woman who almost drown me?

Love Leon

Cassandra's forehead frowned and she sat up instantly, staring at the paper, flipping it back to front and front to back.

She was awake now as she read the letter twice then a third time just to be sure.

"Don't try it," she said to the letter. "You had every opportunity to tell me. How the fuck you gonna come and fuck me then leave on tour? What am I some sort of groupie? You had every chance to tell me face-to-face but you went out like a bitch in some letter... couldn't help yourself? Nah bredrin, you just wanted to get some... I seemed to need something? What the fuck does that mean? Need WHAT? Better this way? What, fucking off in the middle of the night? Act like a couple? Six months yeah?! Alright then... what a dickhead. So EIGHT months of fucking was just fucking to you? Ya damn right, I SHOULD'VE fucking drown you... A fucking letter? Whose gonna fuck me now? Prick done set the bar too high!"

Honouree's Reward

There.

In the midst of a smoky bar sat Tina, staring into her glass of Chardonnay. She was feeling pissed once again because she had been stood up by her boyfriend. She convinced herself the first hour he didn't show that he was simply running late. She phoned his office a million times and got the same response every time.

"Mr Dalton is not in office at this time, please leave a message."

BEEP.

By the time the second hour passed, she made up her mind that she was going to leave. Her suspicions that he was fucking his secretary were further confirmed by his absence, also by the fact that he wasn't doing her.

She flicks her wrist to look at her D&G watch given to her by her mother for her birthday.

It's late and she decides she's had enough. She knocks back her wine and asks the barman to call her a taxi.

It's a Tuesday night so the bar's not full; just regulars, bar flies and voyeurs drinking bottles of beer, a strong scent of weed in the air.

The barman leans over and tells her that her taxi is waiting, while watching her sashay away. She thanks him, briskly walks to the door and is greeted with a stench of rancid hotdogs and burgers.

"Chilly... smells like shit and grease out here," she says to herself, stating the obvious.

She was desperately anticipating the warmth of the taxi and didn't notice the hooded figure creeping up behind her. As she reached for the door of the taxi, he grabbed her handbag, slid it down her arm and knocked her to the ground.

Her instinct is to scream at him, "Give me back my handbag you shit, that's PRADA you cunt."

In her anger, she spied a random brick within arm's reach and hurled it after him but Rounders was never her sport in school.

"Shit... shit... shit... fuck... fuck... fuck..." she cusses tossing her head back in anger, her hair flying around her face, thumping the dirty pavement with her fist.

She feels a heavy breeze pass as a tall man jets past her like Usain Bolt. The man covers a large area in a few strides as he shouts after the tea leaf.

"Oi!"

Mid-stride, he closes in on the teef, grabs his neck and wrestles him to the ground. Prising the bag out his grasp, the tall man stands over the hooded stranger, sweat pouring down his temple.

Without stopping to think, the man drops his foot on the thief's face twice.

"That's a lady, you don't rob ladies, prick."

Walking away from the moaning thief, and the crowd surrounding him, he walks back to Tina, who is still watching from the floor.

He walks right up to her, directly under the glow of the street light, aided by the headlights of the waiting cab.

His skin is mocha, not too dark, not too light, jus' right.

"I think this belongs to you miss," the helpful stranger said, handing her the bag and offering his hand.

"Thank you, you're a saint," Tina responded, slipping her hand into his.

She felt the air being sucked out of her as he strongly pulled her to her feet with no effort.

Rubbing her ankle, she took the opportunity to look at him face-to-face and she wished she didn't as she could feel her panties moistening.

"Did you hurt your foot?" he asked with concern in his voice.

He swings open his floor-length coat and crouches down in front of her, lifting her injured foot onto his knee.

His hands are soft, with a touch of gristle; works hard but takes care of himself, she thought.

"I think you might have sprained it, but don't worry, it's not broken. Would you like some help to get home Miss?"

The sides of his mouth curved in a dangerous smile and Tina noticed it.

"Tina, my name is Tina."

She was a bit tipsy but held it up well, especially since this out of nowhere, sexy, coffee-flavoured, guardian angel of a man appeared before her.

"Well TINA, would you like help to get to your destination?" he asked with that smile.

She imagined being consumed by his huge arms, laying her head on his chest, running her hands up and down his muscular

arms.
 Not that she was a cheater but she desperately missed the caress of a man who knew what he was doing.
 "No I'll be fine," she lied. Her body was screaming for her to throw him into the cab with her but, in today's London, dem tings can't run.

 "Thank you for being a hero, most people 'round here just WATCHED me get mugged, so thank you."
 He knelt down in the open door of the cab and held her hand between his. "That's alright Tina, good thing I was here."
 Closing the door and tapping the roof, the cab pulled into the traffic before Tina could even think to ask the hero his name.

 Home.
 Tina wrestled with her door key and was greeted with an instant cold across her body, not physically but emptiness. Loneliness began to seep through ever since her boyfriend started coming home from work late or not at all. He WAS a busy man, but she knew what he did for a living and couldn't understand how he had to stay late all the time, yet his colleague's wives reported their husbands' home on time.
 She hobbled through the house, kicking her shoes off in frustration. Her first destination was the bathroom for an ankle support, but the flashing light on her answering machine drew her attention. Kissing her teeth, she cancelled her plan of action and two-stepped to the kitchen for a drink... a STRONG one.
 Granted she knocked back a few glasses of Rosé earlier, she was now in the mood for the fiery rum she kept in the cupboard.

 With a quarter-full glass of Wray and Nephew's fire water, she made her way to the bathroom as her ankle turned from a minor ache to an annoying throb.
 Sipping and screwing her face, she turned off her thoughts in the dark bathroom for a moment. She thought about crying, falling apart and curling up on the bed and not answering her phone for the next month. Just turning the fuck off and being alone.
 "Fuck that, fuck him," she said to herself as she turned on the light and ran herself a bath.
 Mixing bath salts and bubble bath, Tina steamed up the bathroom, disrobed and let the sting of the hot water remind her

that she was alive.

She sighed heavily and reached for her drink on the toilet seat.

While the white rum stung her chest, she couldn't help but think about the handsome hero who, literally, came out of nowhere and was gone just as fast.

And all while she was waiting for HIM. Where the fuck was he? Seeing another man do what her man was SUPPOSED to do showed her just how WOTLESS he really was.

God let me see that for a reason, she thought.

After a solid hour of skin shrinkage and confused thoughts of her now EX-man and the hero who took her breath away, Tina washed off, dried off and, with ankle support fitted, went to bed.

The side lamp revealed a spliff HE rolled for when he came home from work.

She lit it with a smile and refused to think about him. She found the thoughts about her face stamping stranger more enticing, and more BEDROOM, thanks to the high grade.

Her nipples rose as if he was sucking them, her mind told her. The curve of her back arched as if he was bending her over doggy style and holding her open.

She was strangely moist before but she was more than wet now as her mind commanded her body to think about his long dick caressing the inside of her pussy.

With the spliff in the ashtray creating a haze, Tina had one hand between her thighs and one in her mouth, making her fingers wet for nipple play.

She worked in a wax on, wax off motion with her hands and was writhing on the bed, bathed in a low light.

Before she could really get going, she felt her stomach tense up and her breath get faster as she came. She hadn't even alternated nipples yet.

She rolled her thighs over the small wet patch she created, took a long toke on the spliff in the ashtray and savoured the draw: inhale, inhale, inhale... hold it... hold it... hold it... exhale slowly.

A Lil' Kim lyric crossed her mind:

"Inhale dis, clench ya fist, can ya' feel the mist though the uterus?"

Fully high and relaxed, she forced herself up and turned the TV on.

DVD?

She pushed his Seinfeld DVDs aside and reached for her favourite film, Pandora's Box.

She always loved that film but HE never did. He couldn't just let go of the reality and just watch the film for what it was.

Can you believe that shit, PANDORA'S BOX wasn't stimulating enough for him? She thought.

While the film loaded, she cursed herself for wanting a cup of tea. She knew that too much movement was no good for her ankle but she went anyway. Her herbal tea and rum knocked her out before Tyson Beckford took the screen with his chocolate goodness.

She woke up to the smell of coffee and clinking in the kitchen. With a rum headache and wine wooziness, she sat up slowly, put on her dressing gown and hobbled on her good foot down her Edwardian staircase.

Her face was a picture of confusion as she picked up a large umbrella and held it over her head.

The intruder in her kitchen was the intruder in her life as her boyfriend stood over the stove, flipping a pancake, with eggs, toast and coffee sitting on her breakfast bar.

"What the fuck are you doing in my house?" she asked.

"Babe, before you say anything, I'm so sorry I got caught up at work."

Tina glared at him and she visualised herself punching him, giving him a well deserved combo like she was Bruce Lee's secret understudy.

"More like you got caught up in your secretary's pussy. Nigga don't even speak, jus' get the fuck out my yard, ah wah? You muss tek dis ting for hotel, you mus' tink sey I'm a fool!"

"But sweetness, let me explain, I left you a message..."

The umbrella was still in her grasp as the sight of him made her ankle ache more. Did he think a hearty breakfast would change her mind? He must've known he fucked up otherwise he wouldn't have snuck in and started on an 'apology' breakfast.

"Derek jus' get your cheating arse out my yard," Tina shouted as she picked up his cold Supermalt and shoved it into his hand.

"So it's like that yeah?" he asked, dashing the spatula into the sink. "Well maybe if you free up more ah di' pum pum, I wouldn't have to be fucking my secretary, would I?"

"If you was any good at fucking, maybe you'd be getting more of it. Do you know what happened to me last night you selfish fucker? Huh?"

She was pushing him out the door while screaming at him.

"I was mugged while I was waiting for you and where was you? Fucking your pawg secretary."

Tina was bellowing at the top of her lungs as she pushed him out the door, shoving him so hard he fell to the ground.

She slammed the door in his face and sat by her breakfast table, so angry that her whole body was shaking.

She looked at the table of food and the pancake burning on the stove. She turned it off, walked past the spread and went upstairs.

Tina needed to get out.
Away from the house.
It smelled of him.

She didn't care where she was going; she just wanted to be out the house. A trip to the book shop would take her mind off her problems, if only for a while.

Tina showered and judged the weather fine enough for her cute white tennis skirt and skin-tight long sleeve top. She loved the way the top was revealing enough to show what colour her bra was. She slipped into her Pastry trainers, jacket, keys, handbag and she was out of the house.

By the time she reached the book shop, she had transformed her limp into a semi-sexy stroll. Heading straight for the black literature section, Tina was a woman on a mission.

Her choice had to be enthralling, enticing, yet exotic enough to hold her attention and take her away from the BITCH her life was about to become after Derek.

Scanning spine-to-spine, she was lost in a world of words when she felt a strong hand on her hip.

"Excuse me," a voice said from behind her.

Tina turned to the left and saw the shadow of a man who was now on her right.

She instantly recognised the strong back of the stranger from last night.

"Hi," she managed.

He turned and his mere presence made her ankle feel weak under her.

"How you feeling this morning? Why are you on your ankle?" he asked.

"I had to..." she started to say. Was she about to disclose her business to a complete, but highly attractive and muscular, stranger? "I just wanted to get some books before staying in for the day."

"Okay."

An uncomfortable silence fell between them, similar to the knowing glance they shared last night.

"You know, I never asked you your name sir."

"Oh, NOW you ask? I hope you don't go 'round talking to random men. It's dangerous out here you know? Some REAL weirdos on road."

"I know, I have a swollen ankle to prove it. So, what's your name?"

"Royston. Royston Hendricks."

"Hendricks!"

"Yeah, different spelling, no relation, trust me I checked."

"Okay, so, Royston? Have you had breakfast?"

Fiddling a book between her fingers, she enjoyed looking up at Royston as he lorded over her, all big and able to pick her up if he wanted to. Tina was enjoying it so much that she didn't realise she just invited him for breakfast. And she didn't mean a Sausage and Egg McMuffin.

"Yes I have, but I'm building an appetite for a snack," he said seductively licking his lips. Tina knew what was on his mind because it was on hers.

Damn, she wanted breakfast, brunch, lunch, tea, supper and some midnight snacks too.

"Well, I've got breakfast at home if you're HUNGRY."

Tina couldn't be stopped and she didn't want to stop herself. She wanted what she wanted and she was going to get it. She wanted that reminder of what it felt like to feel good.

"Breakfast? With you? That would be good."

They paid for their books and walked to a BMW Z4 parked nearby.
"Shiiiit, is that how your rolling?" Tina beamed in amazement.
"You like?" he said proudly.
"What do you think? YEAH!"
Admiring the glamorous vehicle, she imagined herself driving it; wind blowing in her hair, music playing while getting her pussy sucked.
Shhhiiit, she thought to herself.
She didn't rule it out ever happening.

He drove the car with major control which made Tina's nipples hard just watching him. He was fast but not dangerous and when he arrived at her place and parallel parked in one swift movement, Tina knew breakfast was going to be good.
Royston walked behind her into the kitchen, the midday sun creeping though the unopened curtains.
It was an old house with modern touches, classic but stylish. Tina flicked the kettle in the kitchen and Royston followed.
"Sit down, what would you like?" she asked bending over to pull the laces from her trainers.
Royston couldn't resist a peek at her lace French knickers which grinned from below her skirt. As he inspected, he rubbed the side of his dick, which was already semi-hard.

"A dat mi wan," he mumbled.
"Excuse me?"
Standing upright, twisting her back to look at him, she was not expecting him to be that forward with her. Royston sized her up and down, wondering if she could actually handle the package he had for her.
"What the fuck you looking at, you sizing me up or something? Huh?"
"Maybe," he answered.
She could hear that he was in his mode; it was woman verses beast and he was planning to tear her up.
And Tina was in the mood to let him.
"What you tink sey you can handle dis here?" she said

clapping her backside.

That was all Royston needed to hear. He grabbed her arm and pulled her into his huge frame. He wrapped his arms around her and grabbed her arse.

Tina was instantly taken and her pussy was soaking as he smashed his lips into hers and gave her one of THOSE kisses.

Tina had not felt a kiss like that since she can't remember when. Her ex-HE couldn't really cut it as a kisser but she played the part and made do.

Tina needed a good fuck, plain and simple, and she knew she was gonna get one.

She felt his wood poking against her pelvis and all she could think was 'oh God'.

Royston turned her round to face the breakfast bar, pushed her forward, dragged her Frenchies down to her ankles and kissed her neck. Soft and smooth, he trailed down the nape of her neck, down her spine and then he buried his face into her soaking pussy. He tasted every part of her sweet goodness she had to offer.

He traced his tongue on the crack of her arse dipping his tongue into her pussy, spreading her cheeks so he could get all the way in. She pushed back onto his face, grinding her hips.

"Jesus, that feels good," she uttered.

She was enjoying every moment, as he changed it up and slid a finger into her pussy.

"Oh shit, that feels better," he added another and another until he was using three fingers on her, the warmth of her pussy inviting him.

Tina knew that Royston had her already and she knew she was ready to pop her juices.

He pulled away as the feeling got good. He must've known she was close and decided not to let her get an easy one.

Tina turned around; stood him up and fell to her knees until she was face-to-groin. Her white top was discarded onto the kitchen floor as she licked her lips in anticipation.

He released his belt buckle as she fished for his hard wood in his boxers. She had to dig deep to find the end of him and that made her smile.

She flopped him out and took him into her mouth, caressing her tongue all around the shaft, savouring every taste. She licked the top of his dick, sucking it softly as he leaned back, pushing her head further into his dick.

He ushered her to deep throat and she took the whole 15 inches (well that's what it felt like) in her throat as he held her head and face fucked her.

Tina's dribbling everywhere, mouth water all over his dick, balls, her chin and tits as she tastes his pre-come. She lets it coat her tongue and purrs at the sweet taste.

Standing like she can't wait any more, he lifted her onto the breakfast bar pushing all the plates of eggs and toast aside like the Red Sea parting. He lined his dick with her sopping pussy and eased inside her while she moaned. The anticipation alone almost made her come.

He slowly stirs her coffee, working her in... working it... working it round and round.

Royston was hitting every spot in her pussy making her moan.

"You like? Yeah, you know you like this," he gloated with a big grin on his face.

He enjoyed watching her ugly faces as he held her neck and squeezed with a bit of pressure.

"Uuurgh... yeah... that feels good... fucking GOOD... fucking great..."

She grinds her hips into him and he speeds up, his stride deeper and longer, pounding her pussy.

Stroke, stroke, stroke, never losing his stride.

He picks her up from the breakfast bar with her legs wrapped around his body. He holds her arse, lifting and dropping it onto his dick

"Whose the man? You never had good dick like this..."

"Oh shit... yes... right there... ummm..."

He had the biggest grin on his face. That was until she jumped down, turned around and bent over until her palms were flat on the floor. She spread her legs, cocked up her arse and he entered her deep and slow.

Tina moaned.

"Ooooo... ummm..."

He kept it at a steady pace as she pushed back, smashing her pussy into his long wood. Royston watched his wood sliding in and out her pussy and he liked the way it glistened with her juices. He sped up the pace which sent him into a trance with sweat pouring down his face, dripping down the crack of her arse, adding to the flow from her pussy.

She was pumping hard now, smashing her arse into him.

Her body suddenly stiffened and she dropped to her knees, taking Royston with her. Arching her back, she paused so Royston could feel her pussy contracting on his dick.

Her pussy is slippery, his nuts are wet and breakfast and broken plates surround them on the floor.

He keeps pounding then slips it out and massages her arse with it as she looks back at him and gives him the 'okay' by backing her tight hole onto his dick.

Slowly... it's tight... but nice.

"Shiiiit..."

Royston calls out. He can't resist a pump. He does it again... And again.

Tina moans. She hadn't had good sex like this in a long time and she even forgot about her ankle the way she was being thrown around and manhandled.

Tina was ready to cum again as Royston slipped three fingers so deep into her pussy, she sung a long melody of cum all over his hand.

He felt his nuts bubbling again and he couldn't hold it. He withdrew and pumped his seeds all over her arse. Tina turned her head to look at him, his stomach is corrugated and sweat pours down his chest between his pecs and down his stomach to his curly pubic hairline.

He lets out a grin from ear-to-ear as Tina stretches the feeling into her legs.

And her throbbing ankle.

"Imagine that for a hero's honouree award?" She said laughing.

"Yeah, imagine that, there would be hero's everywhere if the reward was good pussy like that." Royston stated.

"So... do you still want that snack or you cool?" Tina asked still smiling. "Yeah... I'm famished."

Royston and Tina continued to have brunch together, sometimes breakfast in bed, or lunch and dinner.

Tina hasn't quite finished thanking him yet.

Marcus and the Truth

It was a cold-ass winter and Marcus didn't want to drive, he wanted to be where Nicola was; sitting in the passenger seat with her hands flat against the heater. But he lost the toss and had to alternate each hand against the heater, while controlling the car.

This just made him angrier as he drove through Kilburn's empty streets, speeding and getting faster with every red light he jumped.

The fact that she was so warm and toasty in front of the heater vent that she took off her winter coat annoyed him even more.

This anger was sitting on top of his aroused pleasure that was awoken just a couple hours ago but sitting in silence in the car, he was forced to choose which to feel.

He thought himself a pretty open-minded guy with a candid look at everything, including sex. But what she did was nothing short of disrespectful and rude, but at the same time, erotic, amorous, electric, forbidden and DEFINTAELY a first for him.

All he wanted to do was have a nice couple's dinner but that turned into Freak Night At the Peckham Apollo.

"Aren't you gonna say anything?" Marcus said with his eyes on the road, cutting through Kilburn like a speed demon possessed.

"What do you want me to say? Want me to apologise, 'cuz I can't do that. You wouldn't want me to do that."

She sounded like his ex-girlfriend Roz when she spoke to him in that way. Trying to sound sincere but managing to sound insincere at the same time.

His anger was saying left and his libido was saying right but his eyes saw straight and he was all over the place.

"Okay," he said, nodding in anger. "OKAY then!"

The car was silent as they sat in their own spaces, their eyes observing the south London scenery but their minds joined somewhere else.

Music was cut off half an hour ago as Jenny Francis spun love song after love song through the airwaves.

And Marcus was not impressed.

The engine hum allowed Marcus to replay just what the hell happened.

Somewhere Marcus never thought he'd go. Somewhere he never thought SHE'D go. What was she doing?

Deep in the heart of Peckham, hours earlier, Marcus and Nicola were clearing a table of dinner plates. Having been invited round for dinner by married couple Simon and Lindsey, they felt it only right that they clear the table.

With the dishwasher loaded, they giggled their way to the living room, whispering to each other about what they wanted to do to each other when they got home.

This wasn't helped by the mutual groping session they engaged in as they both bent over to load the dishwasher.

Jill Scott's Crown Royal played with the incense smoke in the air and softly hazed the room.

"What you two giggling about?" Simon said, sitting on a solo leather chair with Lindsey between his legs on the floor.

"Sex," Nicola answered honestly, falling with her man into the opposite leather sofa.

Marcus giggled some more, "Nic? Hush ya mout'!"

"Why? It's what I want isn't it?"

"Yeah but... you don't need to let the world know."

Marcus felt his dick shrinking with embarrassment.

They'd known Simon and Lindsey a few months and they were trying 'couples night' and this was their third date with the caramel couple.

For Marcus and Nicola, it was an opportunity to get out of the house and interact with other people because they had begun to show signs of that stage in their relationship where they started to 'annoy each other'. For him it was her ability to make everything about the fact that he MAY cheat on her. And her grievance was the fact that she could TELL that he wanted to cheat on her.

Marcus never did but Nicola felt that a man so in touch with his sexual side HAD to be a serial cheat.

The energy of watching Simon and Lindsey interact seemed to ignite a spark in them as she nestled under his arm and enjoyed her body on his.

"So Nicola, you said you wanted sex? Is my man Marcus not sorting you out?" Simon asked.

Marcus smiled then frowned. He had just sat down and they were already knocking his sex. He looked down at his dick and smiled again, just to confirm that there was nothing wrong with his performance.

"No, it's not that, it's just, we just... you know you want the man to be in control right Linds?"

"Oh hell yes... I love it when Simon flings me about the place like a rag doll."

"Exactly... and I love that but, with Marcus, it's ALL the time. I mean, it's not that we're not adventurous, trust me, we've tried some tings, but, I never get a turn to drive the Veyron, you know?"

Marcus' eyes shot open as he heard Nicola open up about their sex life like it was a description of a TV show. He wanted to put his hands over her mouth but he couldn't lift his hands, he was too stunned.

"...I mean, we switch it up regular, but when it gets DOWN to it, he always takes control. Like, can't a sister tek de wheel?"

Nicola, sitting at a sturdy 5 foot 7 and blessed with the darkest chocolate skin God every bestowed upon a human being, fondled her fourth glass of Courvoisier with ice.

"I mean, when I'm riding him..."

"Ermm... hello?" Marcus had to let his uneasiness be heard just as it sounded like Nicola was about to go INTO some shit.

"Nah babe, this is a good time to talk about this... we're all grown ups right?"

"I'll drink to that," Simon raised his glass.

"Me too," Lindsey added, clinking her glass with her man above.

"Okay, so... sometimes, I wanna be able to ride you, without you controlling the wheel."

Sitting like a convict in court, Marcus felt like all eyes were on him. Lindsey was shooting glares of 'what a renk man' and Simon looked disappointed... like Marcus was letting the male race down.

"I just..." Marcus started, downing his Cranaranno, a combination of Disaranno and cranberry juice. "I just like it how I like it... and most time, how I like it is how she likes it."

Simon pumped his fist, "she gon' take it how she gon' take it, right? YEAH!"

Lindsey slapped his thigh, "that's usually true but sometimes Marcus, you just have to let go and let someone do something to you."

The advice, plus the alcohol, had his head spinning. Nicola was stroking his face and that felt over nice but he also thought about not being able to let go... what WAS that?

Nicola continued, "It's not SERIOUS babe, but I've been feeling like this for a while."

Marcus cupped her face and kissed her deeply, running his hands across her neck, down her shoulders and pulling her closer.

It was a kiss she hadn't felt in a long time.

Lindsey watched the couple share a tender moment and looked up at Simon who bent down to kiss her. And feel her right breast at the same time.

"Any time you wanna rule me baby, you go right ahead." Marcus answered with a smile.

Thinking about it, Marcus knew that he could work on his control issues but for now, he'd enjoy the night.

"Yaaaaay," Nicola yelped. "Well then..."

Their attention was stolen by Lindsey whose mouth opened and a tiny squeak released into the air. One of her hands was holding a bottle of Stella Artois and the other was moving slowly between her thighs.

She shook her head, brushing her curly hair from her face and clearing her throat as she looked at the two shades of chocolate on the sofa.

"See something you like?" Nicola asked her.

WHAT? Marcus screamed in his mind.

"Keep talking like that and I might have to tell you." Lindsey fired back, tonguing the beer bottle.

She reached back and grabbed Simon erection, through his trousers.

Marcus expected to look to Nicola and see the same look of shock on her face. But as he turned to her, Marcus found that Nicola was no longer in her seat.

Catching up slowly, Marcus watched Nicola's backside in front of him as she crawled across the floor into Lindsey's space.

This was turning into something I would set up, Marcus thought to himself.

She reached Lindsey, who spread her legs in front of her, and kissed her straight on the lips.

Marcus and Simon's eyes met and they both shrugged their shoulders like, 'I don't know either'.

Nicola's hips swirled as Lindsey brought her 'busy' finger to Nicola's lips and she sucked it with a moan.

She turned around and looked at Marcus. "I want you to watch."

"Watch what?" Marcus replied, beginning to feel the mood that was spreading around the room.

"I want you to watch this," Nicola turned back and continued her kiss with Lindsey and joined her in stroking Simon's erection.

Oh, this has turned into some NEXT shit, Marcus thought. How she just gonna grab man's tings like that?

Tracing a finger along Lindsey's crotch, she answered his question. "I want you to sit there, watch me and not move. Can you do that?"

Hell no I can't do that... what the fuck do you think this is? I didn't set this up, Marcus thought.

Marcus couldn't understand how she could offer him a visual list of so many things to get into right in front of him and not get involved. She asked him like 'yes' was his only answer.

Marcus took a moment to duly note her skill of persuasion before thinking of an answer for her almost impossible question.

He sighed as Lindsey ground her hips against Nicola's finger and Simon looked down at the two ladies in his crotch.

"I can," Marcus decided. "But I'm gonna need another drink."

And with that, Marcus was off to the kitchen to make himself a large 'definately-gonna-put-me-over-the-legal-driving-limit' Cranaronno, followed by a long sip. How did this get here so quickly?

Listening to Nicola and Lindsey giggle from the living room fucked with his mind... they had not even broached the subject of threesomes and foursomes, though he was always open to the idea. But to have to watch?

"That's some cuckold ting," Marcus said to his drink. "New breed a man time then I guess."

Marcus backed his drink, made another and was excited to get to the living room to see where things had gone in his absence.

They had definitely gone somewhere.

Lindsey's short summer dress was a pile on the floor; next to her earrings and Nicola was down to her birthday suit, fixing herself into a position in between Simon's thighs, with Lindsey sliding her face beneath her open thighs.

Walking in, Marcus thought they looked like a human flamed grilled burger with Nicola as the meat.

She paused to watch him walk back into the room. Her eyes were on him; strong and unhappy at the interruption, forcing him into his seat.

He sat down and held her stare, playing the game. Marcus wasn't silly; he knew that Nicola's sudden urge to play with another couple and force him to watch was an exam with no revision. But that's how she was.

Raise ya then test ya.

He licked his lips, sipped his drink and winked at her to continue.

Game on, he thought.

Nicola smiled her dark coco grin and looked down at Lindsey, who was shuffling herself under her groin, which Marcus knew was wet by now.

Simon undid the zip on his trousers and Nicola fished for his dick. When she found the tip, she looked back at Marcus with a cheeky smile.

"Close but I think you win..."

Simon laughed and Lindsey made a noise as she took her first taste, causing Nicola to increase her grip.

"Don't grip too hard." Simon said.

"Yes daddy..." Nicola replied.

DADDY? Whose daddy? You never call ME daddy! Why don't you call me daddy like that?

Nicola looked down at the work Lindsey was doing on her lower smile. Lindsey, with her dash of milk complexion, licked up and down Nicola's crotch and Marcus could see her tongue disappearing then reappearing between her cheeks. His mind and eyes were torn between watching what Lindsey was doing to her, what SHE was doing to Simon and looking at all three of them in their 'love train'.

His heart was beating in anger, his brow was sweating in nervousness and his erection was up in interest.

Nicola didn't turn to face him as she unsheathed Simon and sucked his head once then twice, waited for him to get hard then blessed him with her deep throat.

"Oh... yes... she's talented like you babe..." Simon said to Lindsey.

Lindsey's reply was mumbled by Nicola's clit that was starting to throb. The taste of Simon's salty pre-cum in her mouth soothed the pulse that was travelling up her midsection.

"She tastes like candy..." Lindsey mumbled.

Simon opened his eyes and looked at Marcus, who was wide-eyed and stoic with the scene that was taking place in front of him.

Nicola's hand on another man's thigh, her other hand running up and down his body, her head turning to the left as she went down and turning to the right as she came up, her soft moans as his dick hit the back of her throat. All these things held Marcus' attention.

He wasn't angry in a 'what you doing bro' way but in a 'can I join in' way that made him want to jump off the seat and in between Lindsey's legs.

The fact Lindsey still had her high-cut black G-string on turned Marcus on even more because he could see her lips moving against the moist patch of black covering her groin.

With Nicola very busy in Simon's lap and paying him no mind, Marcus leaned forward on the sofa and reached for Lindsey's ankle that was inches away from him, dancing in delight.

"Eat that shit Linds..." Nicola said, looking down to her pussy.

He caught the dancing ankle and Lindsey sighed a new rhythm. Taking that sound as a sign to continue, Marcus walked his fingers slowly up her thigh. Each step was soft and deliberate, trying to create a little party for himself. Every inch of creamy caramel skin under his touch was a step closer to somewhere forbidden.

His heart thudded in his chest. The higher he walked, the wetter the terrain became. His fingers were walking and sliding, through Lindsey's rain, up her thighs.

Her other leg was flexing.

Switching his fingers to the inside of her thigh, passing the back of her knee, Marcus was focussed on his journey while Nicola slurped, Lindsey gulped and Simon moaned.

A few steps from where he wanted to be, he suddenly felt eyes on him. Tony Toni Tone's It Never Rains In Southern California was the only thing that could be heard as Simon's moans silenced, Lindsey's slurping ceased and Nicola's burping stopped.

Marcus looked up to see Nicola staring at him with Simon's wet dick in her hand.

"What the FUCK are you doing? Didn't I tell you to sit there and not move?"

Freezing his walking fingers, Marcus looked up and no words came to him. He felt like he was caught doing something he shouldn't. And he liked it.

"I... was... erm..."

"You was just er... erm... er... what? I swear I told you to sit there and not move? Seems like you've moved."

"You're giving and getting yours though aren't you?" Marcus replied, strongly.

"What's your point? I told you sit and... oooooh... ooo... oooweee..."

Nicola looked down at Lindsey who didn't understand the pause and went right back to licking her.

"You can't expect me to..." Marcus held his fingers in place on Lindsey's thigh, just in case Nicola changed her mind about the MADNESS that was going on.

"He's moved hasn't he Simon?" Nicola asked, turning to the dick in her hand.

Bringing his head back from staring at the ceiling, Simon looked at Marcus and smiled.

"Yeah... he's moved... but in his defence, I would've done the same."

Nicola looked down, "he's moved hasn't he Linds?"

Lifting Nicola up and sitting her pussy on her forehead, Lindsey looked down at Marcus, whose fingers were inches away from her bald eagle pussy.

"If I say no, can his fingers keep on walking?"

"Nope... sorry... he's not playing by the rules..."

Nicola began jerking her hand up and down Simon's shrinking manhood. Her saliva squelched between her fingers as she squeezed him back to life, while staring at Marcus with lustful eyes.

"Rules? You wanna talk about rules..."

"AH!" Nicola silenced him and pointed to his empty seat with her eyes.

Before Marcus moved, Nicola turned her head back to Simon's dick and slid herself down Lindsey's face – smile to smile.

Well ain't this a bitch?

He damn sure felt like one. All this freakiness going on and he was, apparently, banned from the festivities? What was it about the way Nicola spoke to him that held his fingers in place on Lindsey's thigh that urged him to return to the sofa?

Marcus didn't question, he responded to the adrenaline pumping through him. Making sure Nicola was busy; he quickly slid two fingers into Lindsey's leaking pussy and watched her whole body rise and drop.

The build up must've been too much for her and she groaned into Nicola's pussy, who took the extra pressure on her clit to grind her hips. At the same time, her deep throat velocity had Simon squirming in his seat; not sure whether to watch or look away.

Marcus was back in his seat and with Lindsey's scent on his fingers; he had his souvenir from the festival of fun on the hardwood floor before him.

Lindsey kicked out her leg and moaned as her hand rested on her stomach and her middle finger rubbed up and down furiously beneath her wet thong.

Marvin Gaye's Since I Had You swam smoothly behind them as Marcus stared at Lindsey and her finger work. Nicola in Simon's lap was getting annoying, mainly because he could do with some 'special attention' and the fact she was giving it to someone else was a jar on top of an annoyance.

"You like that Simon? You like that deep all the way down the back of my throat?"

With her face covered by Nicola's deep dark caboose, Lindsey was a pair of caramel breasts, thick, but not fat, stomach and legs which were electric sliding across the floor.

Her mouth must've been working because Nicola was raising off Lindsey's tongue and sliding down onto it... and that meant she was in her zone.

It was messing with his mind, among other things, to watch Nicola doing her thing from a spectator's point of view.

In the past, Marcus and Nicola tried, and mastered, the art of making good home porn, acknowledging simple touches such as lighting and good camera position, but, watching it live, and created by someone else, was something else.

Watching her riding like a bandit on Lindsey's face while using the pleasure and forward momentum to cause Simon immense pain, judging by the look on his face, Nicola gave and received with ease.

Look at my baby go...

Nicola had Simon, literally, by the balls and controlled the pleasure he received by sucking and stopping, enjoying the effect she was having on him. Every now and then, she'd look back at Marcus to make sure he was watching.

And he was watching.
Everything.

Simon could squirm no longer as he made his announcement.
"Keep sucking it like that and I'm gonna come. Can I come in your mouth?"

Chewing Simon in her mouth softly and turning her head, Nicola looked at Marcus, catching him off-guard.

Caught sipping his drink, he coughed and spluttered as Nicola stared at him.

Well...

"If you're gonna do a job, might as well do it properly."

Simon's grunts were his co-sign of Marcus's words and he grabbed the back of Nicola's head and forced himself deep into her mouth. She winced and adjusted her throat to accommodate him. She shook her head from side-to-side to slide him in further and Simon let go of her head and the door to his restraint.

"Make me come lady lick a lot..." Nicola mumbled.

Marcus was mesmerised by Nicola's throat control and the

way she made it comfortable, with a simple head turn. Granted Simon wasn't the same size as Marcus but she handled it just the same.

Make him buss' baby...

"Ooooooh shiiiiit..." were the only words Simon could muster.
Nicola suddenly sucked up his shaft, allowed his geyser to erupt then dropped her mouth so fast and deep, her lips reached his balls.
Marcus was as hard as he could get, bursting against his loose jeans. Watching Nicola take the shot, while deep-throating, showed the talent to take it there, swallow and make it look easy.
Simon lay back like someone had let the air out of him. He was shouting all types of inaudible obscenities into the air and was screeching as he shrunk in Nicola's still busy mouth.
"Marcus... mate... you're girl's a KILLER..."

Nursing his drink, Marcus half-smiled at Simon, who stood up while spanking Nicola, making her behind giggle for, at least, three seconds.
Marcus was surprised that his half smile was filled with sympathy for Simon, who had to endure Nicola's text-book perfect head... and was screaming like a banshee afterwards.

Sipping from Lindsey's drink, Nicola was bouncing roughly on her face, lost in an alternate universe, while her body slow flowed like it was under water. Marcus looked at Simon, adjusting his flaccidity into his zip. He expected to harbour more anger towards Simon after what he just saw, but Nicola made him come hard and Simon looked like he was walking wounded.
Just the way Simon was swaying said that he was more than weak in the knees.
Sylvia Striplin's You Can't Turn Me Away grooved Simon to his knees as he climbed on top of Lindsey's writhing body.

Where else could this go?

Simon ran his hands up and down Nicola's back and her body reacted to his touch. She stretched herself out onto the seat Simon occupied as he spread Lindsey's thighs as wide as the sky, her love scent swelling through the room.

Nicola turned her face to Marcus as she ran her pussy up and down Lindsey's face, grinding her teeth and hips at the same time.

Her face was intense.

His eyes were locked with hers.

She was asking him a question with her strong growl.

"Harder..." Marcus commanded.

Nicola stood up suddenly, while Simon licked his way down his wife's body. She went into the splits and lowered herself back onto Lindsey's waiting, moaning face, all while keeping her eyes on Marcus.

And Marcus only.

She leaned over Lindsey's face and fucked her tongue.

"More... more... more..." Nicola demanded, winking at Marcus.

"Give her more..." he said.

Simon was the first to react and immediately slid up Lindsey's shaking body and joined her in Nicola's pussy.

With Lindsey on clit duty, Simon tongue fucked Nicola's rough movement and held her still.

"Oh that's more... that... umm... is... hmmm... more..." Nicola managed. "Just... do... that...I... want to... come..."

Marcus was ready as she looked over the couple licking her pussy and grinned in his direction, while shivering slightly.

Marcus reacted first. "You wanna come don't you?"

Opening Nicola up and spreading her cheeks, Lindsey and Simon made it impossible for her not to come. Marcus could see her shaking thighs and knew that she was two train stops away from satisfaction.

"Please..." Nicola pleaded, her eyes straining to stay open, her mouth in a perfect O.

Marcus leaned forward with his drink hand balanced on his knee, spilling liquid on the floor with no-one but Nicola seeing it. And she was 'too close' to care.

Plus it wasn't her house.

"What, now? You wanna come NOW?" he asked.

"OH YES... right now... right now... right now... right... now..." she rapidly repeated.

"You gonna squirt on that poor woman's face aren't you?"
"OH... MY... GOD... I... AM... look... please..."

Marcus enjoyed this game. His control had returned just in time for Nicola's almighty orgasm. She'd had a few small ones here and there, he noticed, but she was yet to have her 'spray the walls' climax.

He scooted across the floor to within inches of Nicola's sweat dripping face, which was squashed in Simon's seat. Lindsey continued to lick the top of her clit while Simon made a sweep from clit to entrance to her asshole and back again.

Marcus just stared at her.

Emotionless, non-smiling, alien stare.

Nicola was squinting, moaning and winking as her hips were held down and forced to take what was being given to her.

"You ready baby?"

"Yes..." Nicola replied quickly. "Yes... yes... yeeeeees..."

"So what you waiting for?" Marcus said, whispering.

She closed her eyes and tried to manoeuvre enough space in Simon's grip to move her hips. Shaking like a cold animal, Nicola's mouth opened but no sound came out.

"You wanted to come didn't you? Come then..." Marcus said, his delivery sinister and frosty.

Nicola's eyes smiled and she let out a shrill scream as she shook in Simon's grasp, Lindsey's face a rubbing board for her pussy.

Marcus leaned back and took them all in: Nicola fused with the top of Lindsey's body, with Simon laying on top of her with his face replaced by Nicola again.

"Y...e...s... I... did... yeeeees I am..."

She pounded the hell out of Lindsey below as her pussy audibly released, spraying over Simon's shoulder, splattering the leather sofa where Marcus was perched.

Lindsey gurgled and Simon's face emerged dripping from the shower as Nicola – still staring at Marcus – hummed a sweet soul melody while her thighs were on some funk shit.

A stream ran between Lindsey's breasts while Nicola chased her breath which was keeping its distance.

"Yeah?" Marcus asked.

"Oh yes... definitely yes..." Nicola said, her voice as shaky as her body. "A thousand times yes..."

Pulling his soaking partner from under Nicola, Simon cupped her face and kissed her. Their wet faces were sliding together as they hummed and groaned in the kiss.

Nicola was still face first in Simon's seat and still shaking.

"You came?" Marcus asked with a smile.

"YOU... moved?" Nicola asked back, still attempting to catch her breath.

Office Tales

Dante sat at his desk with his morning mocha, with a sprinkle of brown sugar. Looking around the empty office, he sipped quickly before the sting of the heat caught him and he sighed as he awaited her arrival.

"Oh shit, her drink," Dante said to himself as he jumped up from his desk and ran back to the kitchen to make Naomi's morning cup of coffee in her favourite mug with the slogan: 'Men are like elephants, look good from a distance, but you wouldn't want to own one.'

Measuring a precise half spoon of coffee, with a literal splash of milk, Dante had been on the other end of Naomi's unhappy coffee face before and was not looking for that. Not today.

The way she ran her office, iron fist swinging, meant that to fuck up her coffee was a fail of epic proportions.

As her PA, Dante understood the importance of starting her day off with the right drink, otherwise the whole office could suffer for one coffee grain too many.

Working with Naomi for the past three months was an adventure in itself. Not just as a boss, but a tyrant the way she ran her publishing company. Working to raise the profile of black UK authors, poets and artists, Naomi didn't suffer fools easily and would rather curse you out than shake your hand. Some would call that unprofessional but those people would never dare say it to her face.

And for Dante, today was D-day. The day where he would know, one way or another, if the job was his on a full-time basis.

With her drink ready and her plate of pastries and Krispy Kreme doughnuts, Dante was ready for her imminent arrival.

"If this is my last day, let me get her coffee right."

As the office started to fill, Dante could feel her presence in the building. The air got tighter in the open-plan office, with Naomi's office at the back, so she could oversee everything with Dante's desk and chair in front. Like a good little doggy.

As the lift reached the floor, Naomi walked in on her phone. From the sound of it, whoever was on her line was getting torn a new asshole.

"I don't give a flying fuck who you are or who you work for, but if I tell you my plumbing is not working then I expect you to send someone round right away to fix it. What the fuck am I paying extra for home coverage if you don't cover my home at all times? No... no... no... Monday will NOT do... that means I have to wait a whole weekend for a bath. Are you fucking crazy? You know what, I'm done with you now, can I speak to your supervisor or manager please? Thank you."

Naomi's brown power suit with knee length pencil skirt was sculpted to her hot chocolate frame and finished in Carvela Red heeled court shoes.
She greeted no-one and power walked straight to her office, ignoring Dante's handful or delicacies and slamming the door with her foot.
He stood there holding her coffee out for her but he was also blanked as she continued cursing on her phone.
He looked around, making sure no one watched the blankage, sat down to open an email and started to read it, but knew that ANY second, Naomi would finish on the phone and...

"AL?! COME IN HERE PLEASE."

Picking up her plate of delectables, her coffee and her morning task sheet under his arm, Dante shuffled slowly to her door. He knew the rules and did not knock and instead waited.

"ENTER..." Naomi said.
Dante opened the door and walked cautiously into the IKEA-decorated office, closing the door softly. Naomi was sat behind her king-sized oak desk and was obviously not in a good mood, thanks to the wanker on her phone. He placed her cup of coffee on her Amsterdam coaster and sat down as she turned her computer on and kicked her shoes off.

"Right, this is what I need today. I need that Queenie chick from accounting to get me the contracts for the Samirah project, call Kelly from marketing department, I need to see her speedy Gonzalez. Get me those Quirksville girls to design an advertising campaign for the Karr project, print me out a copy of the meeting minutes with Dizzee, get me Idris's manager on the phone about the biography, tell that cum slut in IT to come and fix my screen..."

Dante's hands were a blur on his BlackBerry as he worked hard to type the last instruction, while trying to remember the one before. He could feel his thumbs straining with each letter he typed, forgetting punctuation and quality and trying to get the quantity of her list down.
God forbid he would have to ask her to repeat herself.
"...call Lexy Harper and get her into my office, get me a menu from that new food place up the road, make sure the conference room is booked for the 1pm meeting with Meg and Annie and please, please, fucking please... could you tell that tramp out

there who thinks her Britney Spears perfume is cute, it isn't."

Dante didn't stop typing until he read the last instruction. For some reason, Naomi was on cold spitting form this morning, her mouth flowing quicker than her brain, all the while sipping her coffee – with no frown – and tearing into a glazed cruller.
With his eyes on his phone, he could feel Naomi's eyes on him; scanning and reading him. But he didn't want to look up at her because he knew whatever mood she was in, she was still going to ask him the question that was currently cutting up his backside.

"So," Naomi started. "Did you do it?"

Dante sighed. "Yes, I did."

"OoOoOoh, lemme see."

And with those words out, Naomi jumped out of her seat, inches shorter than she was when she walked in, and stood in front of him before he could make it to his feet. Reluctance trapped him in his seat as he looked up at Naomi, coffee in one hand and doughnut in the other, and excitement slapped across her face.

"Come on, come on, come on, hurry up..."

"Don't rush me woman," Dante said, forgetting himself.

"Excuse you?"

Dante didn't respond, instead he submitted his will by standing up clearing his throat and unbuckling his belt.
He zipped himself down slowly as she dangled a foot towards his dick.
She skipped back to her chair, reclined it fully, picked up a glazed devil's cake doughnut and looked at him.
Standing there.

"Turn around then."

Doing as he was told, Dante shuffled in his trousers that were cuffed around his ankles, restraining his movement. With his back to her, Dante could only stare at the ceiling, thankful that the blinds in her office were closed.
Though she gave him one of her thongs to put on, when he got home and tried it on, his helmet fell out of one side and his testicles were separated by the string that constantly got caught on the tiny hairs between his cheeks.

I'm at least gonna be comfortable, Dante thought.

A quick visit to Ann Summers where his friend Leslie worked and he had himself a COMFORTABLE male thong which would equally please her, hopefully.

The sound of her excitement at Dante's cheeks in her face told him that she didn't mind that he chose not to wear her thong as she reached out for him and pulled him backwards.
Damn near losing his balance, Dante shuffled backwards towards her, standing there as she felt his cheeks, running her hands up and down his inner thighs, cupping his groin with her hands, sniffing his man scent on her fingers.
Dante turned and watched her hold her fingers to her nose. She hummed to herself, not taking her eyes off him, then sat back, hitching her skirt up as she went.

She shuffled in her seat, fighting to get her panties off, still looking deep into his eyes.
"Come eat this," Naomi said.

With reluctance still in his ether, Dante stepped out of his trousers and watched Naomi push her chair back and spread her legs on her desk.
She pointed between her thighs, threw her panties at him and smiled, "Come on then..."
Dante dropped to his knees as if her voice was crack to an addiction. Walking on his knees, he ducked under her left leg and popped up between her thighs.
He was about to say something but Naomi didn't want to hear anything from the bald caffe latte man between her thighs, she just wanted to feel him. And thus, pushed his head into her crotch with authority.

Breakfast time, Naomi thought.

His first move was his tongue directly on her clit. Hard. No flicking, no swabbing, just a straight poke. Just how she liked it. Her back arched and she gripped the arm rests of her chair with her face to the ceiling. She showed her gritted teeth as Dante put his tongue back in his mouth and replaced it with his lips which exposed her clit, allowing his tongue unobstructed access.
Naomi was in another place and didn't notice her foot swiping at her cup of coffee, which trailed all over her floor.
The sound of the cup hitting the floor broke Dante from his stroke and he tried to turn to the noise but Naomi grabbed his head with both hands and held him in place.
She looked down at him and smiled, "Stay there... no... not there... THERE... that's it... you ARE learning..."
Dante mumbled something unintelligible as Naomi locked her fingers behind his head. He wanted to breathe but the sound she was making was the first sign of an orgasm.

And he wanted that orgasm.

Sucking in small breaths where he could, Dante kept her clit exposed as he alternated between it and her wetness that was now gleaming in his chin beard.

"You really have learned some new.... ooooh..."

Slapping her desk with her hand, Dante noted the 'tap out' but kept going. He knew she was close. He was well aware that one more repetition of his 'clit lick, clit lick, dip inside' would have her dribbling on her leather chair.

"You KNOW I'm close don't you?"

"Yep..."

"You want me to come don't you?" Naomi asked.

"Yes ma'am," Dante said in a faux American accent.

Fully grinding her hips on his face, Naomi started on her slippery road to pleasureville when...

KNOCK KNOCK KNOCK

Naomi's pulling into her groin became pushing as she forced Dante under her desk and slid her legs with him, trying to create equilibrium in her demeanour as she went.

She brushed her hair down, looked in her compact mirror and scanned her desk for any signs of sex – or head.

"ENTER!"

Continually knocking as she entered, Kimisha, the secretary from the downstairs reception, poked her head round the door, with a cheesy grin.

Due to the fact it was first thing in the morning, and she knocked on her door instead of waiting like everyone else, Naomi was already unimpressed by the interruption but, with Dante under the desk, she was frustrated and pissed off as she felt her muscular thighs shaking of their own accord.

Oooh, this bitch better be quick, Naomi thought.

"Morning," Kimisha said, leaning into the office.

From behind her desk, Naomi nodded as so not to give her any impression that she was inviting her in. Kimisha took the nod as her way in and softly closed the door.

As the 5 foot 10 toffee-flavoured woman walked towards the desk, Dante could feel Naomi forcing him deeper under the desk with her thighs. If it wasn't for the strong oak backing of her desk, Kimisha would see him on his knees, thong cutting him in half with the boss's legs knocking against his chest.

"What can I do for you Kimisha?" Naomi asked, trying to keep her

frustration, which was transforming into anger, at bay.
"Well, I seem to remember that your PA Dante is coming to the end of his probation period and you might be looking for a replacement for the job?"
"I might be," Naomi added. "Why you want the job?"
"Well, of course, I'd wait to see if you give the job to him, but if he's not working out then I'd love the job."
"I wasn't offering it to you," Naomi replied, cutting Kimisha off before she got ahead of herself.
Listening intently, Dante rested his arms on Naomi's thighs, indignant that Kimisha was trying to secure the job that she 'hoped he'd get'.
Face-to-face with Naomi's groin, Dante saw the opportunity and manoeuvred himself around her leg and put himself between her thighs.

Hearing her pause from above, Dante trailed both hands up her inner thighs and watched the muscles shiver in response. She tried to close her thighs but he grunted as he pinned them against the inside of his crawl space.
"Look," Naomi started. "Ya boy's got 24-hours to show me something. So let him do his thing and I'll talk to you at the end of the day."
Naomi had no intention of talking to Kimisha and knew she would duck out long before.
Right now, Dante's fingers were unfolding the fat of her lips and making it hard for her to speak.
"So, is there... ANYTHING... else... I can do for you?" Naomi asked, stuttering on Dante's fingers. Each of his digits struggled to keep her open under such moist conditions.
"You alright Naomi? You look hot, is it that time of the month? When I get MY period..."
Naomi slammed the table with one hand and shook everything on it. Her stare was direct and showed that this was not conversation time.

"I... Have some phone calls to make so if you don't mind?"
With her hand showing Kimisha the door, Naomi waited until the amazon-sized receptionist was out of the door before she attempted to slide her chair back.
But her thighs were still locked to the desk.
Dante was brushing his index finger up and down her exposed clitoris with feather-like touches and Naomi's hips were grinding in

her seat.
To anyone who had lost their mind and decided to walk into her office without knocking, the always imposing Naomi would've looked like a fiend in withdrawal.
"Faster..." she huffed.
Down below, Dante puffed a slow breath of warm air onto her thighs as he sped up, per her request.
Naomi was gone.

Sliding up and down in her chair, Naomi ground her nails into her mouse mat and held a long sigh. Her nipples felt stifled under her M&S bra but felt good pressed against the material as her chest heaved.
"That's faster," Naomi hummed, exhaling sweetly to herself.
  The orgasm was quick to arrive and came over her like a sneeze, only better.

Dante pushed her chair and her limp carcass back enough so he could clamber out, thong still cutting him in half.
Standing over her throbbing body, Dante smiled.
"Don't looked so pleased with yourself? I came harder by myself this morning." Naomi said.
Dante scoffed, "In your dreams."
"Exactly. Step up ya game and get to work."

Turning to pick up his trousers, Dante got a firm, five finger slap on the backside, both cheeks.
He didn't need to face Naomi to know that she was grinning, a real conniving smirk that usually surfaced when she was being cold and unwavering in the boardroom.
She hummed a soul melody as he danced back into his trousers, picked up her coffee mug and went to make a start on the massive list he was given.
"Hey Al?" Naomi said, sugar soft with a hint of naughty school girl.
"Yes?" Dante sighed.
He knew his name wasn't Al and every time she called him so, he had the same conversation with himself. He knew damn well she called him Al as in the term for hard pasta; al dente.
Apparently, she liked him hard.

  Why do I keep responding to it, he thought.

"How do I taste this morning?"
"What?"
Standing up, Naomi straightened her shirt and skirt, stepped over the coffee on the floor before walking to within an inch of Dante's flinching face.
She tipped on her toes, grabbed the back of his straining neck and licked his face.
"How does my pussy taste this morning?"
"Kinda milky today," Dante replied.
"I was gonna say fruity but whatever."
Naomi released him as he opened the door and shoulder barged the door-frame so hard, the whole office looked up at him.
Dante sucked a huge breath through his teeth as he rubbed his aching shoulder and fell into his chair.
Licking his lips, he smiled.
"I CAN taste fruit juice."

For the remainder of the day, Dante worked under Naomi's ever-watchful eyes. His list of chores had him up and down the four floors of Naomi's office but he traversed the space without breaking a sweat. That was because he knew the lay of the land very well and, being Naomi's only representative, he walked knowing he was shadowed by the power of her name.
Though the thong he was still wearing was laser beaming through his booty cheeks, he soldiered through.
He played verbal tennis with Melissa from accounting, left a message for Claire from marketing that Naomi needed to see her from YESTERDAY, printed out the minutes from the meeting, got Linda Mills on the phone for EJD, dialled a wrong number for the Quirksville girls and spoke to the cum slut in I.T. about Naomi's screen.

If I get this job, I bet you I'll find out why she's a cum slut, Dante thought to himself.

During a stolen moment at his desk, before lunch, Dante's phone rang and he answered it, hoping it was one of the many people he was awaiting call backs from.
He was wrong.

"Can you still taste my fruit juice?" Naomi asked.
"I told you, it was milky today. You were fruit juicy yesterday,"

Dante remembered.
Yesterday, when she took him to the top floor in the lift, stopped it mid-floor, raised her skirt and put his head under as they ascended.
Naomi loved it. Dante almost suffocated but the power of her orgasm was worth it.

"Do you remember yesterday Al?"
"Yeah, do you?"
"Of course I do, silly boy. Come in here for a minute."
Dante heard that tone of voice before. He knew what that voice wanted, what it desired, what it needed. And he walked strong and proud to deliver it.
With the print out of her lunchtime menu in hand, Dante waited at her door and when she gave him permission, he entered, closing the door.
Naomi was on the phone with her legs up, feet in her Kill Bill slippers and attention on her computer screen.

"Is that my lunch menu?" Naomi asked, with her BlackBerry Torch on her shoulder, blocking the speaker and her fingers, taping on her keyboard.
"Yeah, for that new place that just opened up down near Shoreditch."
"So why are you still holding it?" She whispered as she took it from him.

Eyeing him up and down, Naomi beckoned with her index finger and he approached her desk.
She made him sit on her desk while she continued her conversation with a potential client.
"Yeah, well, that's why you called me. I mean, let's call a spade a spade, you know what we do here and you know we do it well..."
She paused in her flow, allowing the other person to speak as she unzipped Dante's trousers, fishing around for the head of his dick. Once released from his thong, he watched.
Then she sat back and resumed her conversation.
At this point, Dante felt more like a piece of meat than usual. Like his options to zip himself up and complain about such treatment were taken away because:
A) he wanted the job and a 'no' to any of her advances could jeopardise that.

2) He had never been so lucky with a woman of such power and he was totally hooked on it.

As large and as strapping as he was, it was an alien experience for him to be told when and what to do in the way that Naomi did it.
She made it seem like it was his duty to please her the way she demanded. But please her he did.
"You know why you called us. 'Cuz HarperCollins and them man deh, they don't cater for black folk the way we do... Exactly, the product we bring to the table delivers everytime..."
Dante's now erect penis was in her sights as she said the last line and she reached out for it with a strong grip.
Eye-to-eye with his mini-representative, Naomi looked around Dante's frame, through her open door and into her office to make sure everyone was at lunch. And the clockwork way she ran her office, everyone was.
She clicked to speaker-phone as she moved her chair so she spoke within an inch of his helmet.
"Well if you want me to do it, just say so and I'll put the wheels in motion... Uh huh... Yeah, of course you'll be taken care of..."
Dante's dick was a dancing machine and Naomi's voice was the song. He was fighting the desire to wrap his hands in her shoulder-length hair and give her a mouthful of him but, remembering where he was, he fought against it.
With the person on her phone buzzing with business talk, Naomi took him in her palm and squeezed so his head inflated while keeping locked eye contact. He wanted to grimace but he didn't want to give her the satisfaction.
With her eyes burning through him, waiting for a reaction, Naomi lowered her head into his lap slowly.
"Look, right here," she said. "Right now, do you think if you gave me your business and let me take care of you, I'd do a good job?"
Dante nodded. Her phone agreed as she opened her mouth and put it over his mushroom head.
Warm and moist, Naomi enveloped him but didn't touch him. The heat from her mouth and the saliva that dripped down the walls of her cheeks were all she wanted him to feel.
By this point, Dante was wide-eyed and in major shock with what was taking place in his lap. As wet as her handjobs had been in the past, she had never given him head and he hoped this would

be the first.

Wrong again.

Naomi, without warning, slid back on her chair, slapped his dick with her free hand then picked up the menu print out from her desk.
"Just send me the paperwork and we'll get this thing started. But don't mess me about, I don't like to be messed about. Well, sometimes."
Dante watched Naomi with anger on his face and a warm pain fired across his groin. It wasn't like a testicles hit, where the pain took a few seconds to register in his stomach. This pain was instant, straight to the length of him, starting at his head and finishing in his nuts, which lead to the stomach pain.
But Naomi, now scribbling on the menu, was none the wiser.
She handed him the menu, with stars next to her order.
"Take the money out of petty cash and get me a Nigerian Guinness from the corner shop please? Thanks sweet cheeks. Off you go."

And that was it. No recognition of the searing pain in his midsection, or pleasure from a blowjob that she was so close to completing. She just gave him her lunch order and told him to jog on.
Adjusting himself back into his banana hammock, he took £20 from the petty cash tin and waited for the lift, still confused as to why she would get so close to sucking his dick, but not.

Why do that, Dante thought. What's the point? If you wanna suck my dick, just do it innit? I aint gonna stop you am I? You just like to play.

  The lift pinged and he stepped in. Looking up from the floor buttons, he saw Naomi in her office, working on her computer. He stared, hoping she would look up at him before the doors closed.

If she looks back at me then I'll know I'm right about this chick, Dante thought.
Come on, look at me.

Naomi rested on her hands, deep in something as she started

another phone conversation.
She looked up at him with immediate bedroom eyes and a soft smile that spoke volumes. Then the lift pinged and the doors closed.
"Hurry back."

And he did.
 A quick slide to the restaurant and a dip to corner shop and he was back in the office within 15 minutes.
Dante hoped to catch Naomi in the same playful mood but when he stood at her door, her reply was far from sexual.
"Come in, come in, geezusss, hurry up with mi food nah man!?"
She snatched the bag of food from him and ushered him out before she went back to her computer space, opening her Guinness with her teeth.
With his hopeful erection disappointed, Dante opened his lunch at his desk, popped his headphones in and tried not to think about how he felt more attracted to her when she 'handled him'.
From his first day at work, she made her intentions towards him very clear by grabbing his package during a joint lunch date. The first week had him spending late nights in Naomi's presence over the intricacies of contract law and the art of publishing, mixed with soft flirting. By his second month, Naomi had him using his fingers on her at the end of long brainstorming sessions, much to his surprise. And by the middle of month three, she was giving him handjobs during lunch breaks.
All her rules, always her way.

 To watch her in full swing when she was on the phone, dressing down some poor subordinate who dropped the ball was poetry in motion. Naomi was quick witted and armed with dangerous retorts but she also knew her stuff.
Sprinkled with a hot dose of sexuality and the freedom to show it whenever she wanted made Naomi a drug.
Her control over him made him question his masculinity once or twice but he was lost in the way she was.

Lost in his own thoughts and moving, machine-like, through his chore list, Dante didn't realise it was the end of the day.
Ruing the fact that he didn't manage to get through his list, Dante finished sending his last email and logged off. Hopefully, not for the last time.

Like clockwork, his work BlackBerry buzzed and he had a message from Naomi.

"Could you come into my office please? And lock the door as you come in. It's time for your evaluation."

Standing at her door, Dante brushed himself down and tried to mentally prepare himself for a final conversation.
Pushing the door, he was presented with Naomi, in all her chocolate naked splendour, sitting cross-legged on her desk. Dante closed and locked the door and turned to face her with an uncontrollable smile.
Over his three months at Naomi's front desk, he had seen many parts of her naked but never the whole package. He stood for a moment in awe.
Such power, such beauty, such a woman!

"Come sit."
"You do realise that..." Dante stuttered.
"I'm naked, yes... it happens all the time."
Dante recoiled, "Nah, its just I've... You know what, don't worry..."
Naomi hopped off her desk and waited for Dante to get close to his seat before brushing her naked self past him, the effect taking hold instantly.
Sitting with his legs apart, his dick imprinted against his thigh, he watched her walk to her chair.
Naomi fell into her chair with her legs crossed on the desk and his file in her lap.
"So, let's have a look at what we have here. Okay, Dante... Ha ha, that rhymes. Silly me... Anyway, Dante... Ha ha, I did it again..."
"Did you bunn a fat head this afternoon?"
"Maybe... But cha, its my company, and if I wanna go out for a spliff walk on a Friday afternoon, then I will..."
"Do you innit!?" Dante agreed. No point rattling her cage so high in the sky when she held his career in her hands.
"Tell me Dante," Naomi said, coming over all serious. "What has it been like for you working here over the last three months?"
"What? Are you seriously gonna sit there looking all sexy and naked and ask me 'bout work?"

Dante was ruffled. Usually the games Naomi played were

adaptable into his own sexual practices, some were even his fantasies. But, deep down, he hoped that every sexual situation they found themselves locked in over the last few months would lead up to him actually getting some.
He played along; he was always a willing participant to her any-time, any place random call. He always gave 100% effort when it came to giving her head, didn't even ask for head in return, even though she teased him with it. So why the big final game?

If this is gonna happen, then I'm gonna make it happen, Dante thought to himself.

"What did you just say to me?"
The low mood lighting which gave her office a sexy glow upon entry, now looked sinister as Naomi stared at him with frown lines across her brow.
"Game time is over..." he added. "I want you, you want me, so let me find what it's like to slide inside ya."

Naomi's sinister grin silenced Dante as he felt a large shift of energy come his way. He watched her slowly close the folder in her lap, tap a few buttons on her computer, pull out her iPad and connect it up.
Before the first download started, Naomi, like a cat, quickly pushed back on her chair, hopped onto the desk and kicked the headrest of his chair.
   It happened so quick, he didn't have time to register what she was doing until he felt the chair start tipping backwards.
Connecting with the chair sweetly, she made him flip backwards. His legs and erection went over his head and he slid away from the chair on the floor.
Before he could look up to figure out what that FUCK just happened, Naomi was on top of him. It was like she was more than upset that he tried to take control of her situation.
And she suddenly turned into Catwoman.

But that drop kick thing was serious, Dante thought.

Naomi slapped his file to the floor near his head before ripping his shirt open, exposing his chest. The sight of his sand-coloured skin tone seemed to enrage her more as she made quick work of his belt.

"Game time is NEVER over AI."
She pulled his belt out of his trousers with one yank and whipped the ground with it.
"I haven't even started with you. Now..."
Naomi spun around and sat on his chest while removing his trousers and thong.
"...that's better... Now, let's talk about your progress Mr AI Dante..."
Spinning back on his chest, she sat her pussy so close to his face that he could pout and taste it.
"You wanna give me my appraisal with your pussy right..."
"RIGHT THERE!" Naomi finished. "Now, I spoke to all the members of staff you've worked with and they have all said that you're a joy to work with, intelligent, willing to learn, creative, perceptive..."
With each word of praise, Naomi rubbed her pussy. It was as if she was reading an instruction manual on masturbation the way she flicked through the pages.
"I like it here," Dante said, watching little drops of her rain fall.
"The people you have in your company know what they're doing, they understand the market, the know how to reach that market and I think you really have a good thing going here and I wanna be a part of it."
"Good answer."

Her computed made an 'uploaded' sound.

Naomi hopped off his chest and scuttled to her iPad. Snatching the device off her desk, she hopped right back to her throne like she was never gone.
"Okay, we're gonna play one more game."
"I told you, I'm done with the games. If your gonna give me the job then just give it to me. If not then, thanks."
Dante attempted his own jedi mind trick and made sure he said 'just give it to me' with the right tone.
"Don't try and play slick with your tone AI. And for the record, you HAD the job from week one, all this stuff has just been entertainment for me."
Dante sighed, "Thank you for giving me this opportunity."
"I may have offered you the job but you don't have it yet. And that's where my game comes in. And if you can win this game, then the job is yours. In fact, I'll even raise your salary. Deal?"

Dante's mind went blank.
Such an offer, with her pussy leaking on his chin beard, was a brain buster.
Naomi was not a simple woman to begin to understand. Because, not only was she clever, but she was astute and coupled with an obvious dirty streak, she was not a woman who took the word 'no' easily. Not once did Dante ever enquire why she was this way or which man may have made her this way.

Maybe he could find out.

But whatever it was, Naomi was now planted on his chest, reaching round for his dick, which was limping between her fingers.
"This game is in two stages. I'm gonna show you a set of pictures and I want you to look at these pictures and tell me what you see. If you look at these pictures and you get turned on, then I'll get turned on. If I get turned on, then you will get to fuck me. NOW...IF you get to fuck me..."
"There's more?" Dante asked.
"IF you get to fuck me, then you need to make me come. If you can do that, the raise is yours."
Dante thought for a moment, "You REALLY like to do things differently don't you?"
"Makes it interesting, wouldn't you say?" Naomi asked as she rubbed her pussy over his mouth, allowing a long strain of juice to snap into his mouth.
"Okay, let's do it," Dante agreed sucking up.

Naomi unwrapped a condom and shuffled down to his knees, where she would listen and wait, ready to pounce on the erection when it surfaced.
"What's this?" She asked him, handing him the iPad.
Staring at the photo, in the warm light, Dante could make out two shapes. One laid back in a leather reclining office chair, another in between their thighs.
"It's... me and you! Whoa, hold on, that was in here. You mean you took photos of us? Where?"
Naomi slapped him softly as she chuckled, "Focus Dante, there's an orgasm at stake here."
"It looks like me fingering you in your chair, with your legs in the air after you got the triple ladies account."
"Correct. Next."

Dante scrolled his finger on the photo and another one took its place.

In the next photo, Naomi was face down, ass up on her desk and Dante was face first sitting in her chair.

"That was after the office party, when you climbed on your desk in that rah-rah skirt and told me to 'find the treasure'. That was a fun game."

Down below, Dante's penis showed it's first signs of life. It went from limp to semi-erect right before her eyes and she clapped her hands together.

"That was the first time I face fucked you." Naomi said seductively.

You called? Dante's erection said to her.
That was all she needed.

Unbeknowst to him, Naomi wanted him just as bad but she was the boss; she had a reputation to uphold and if a fine man like Dante was going to walk into her office, she would keep him or make him limp out.

Naomi grabbed the iPad from his hands and tossed it on the sofa. As she turned to face him, Dante was upright and in her personal space. He cupped her face and kissed her deeply.

Though she tried to resist, his lips were five-star hotel duvet soft. She kept her lips rigid but he continued to kiss her lips, with his hips jerking below.

With her lips responding to his kiss, and her pussy moistening, Naomi wrapped her arms around his shoulders and secured him in place.

She never really took the time to kiss Dante and from the looks of things, she missed out.

He was soft and adapted well but he also read the moment and knew when it was time to take control.

Naomi could feel her stomach tingle as her tongue probed for his. During her search, Dante wrapped his arms around her body and squeezed as he pumped his hips, forcing himself as far into her as possible.

She moaned into his mouth while her nails pressed into his face. Quiet yelps of pleasure rumbled in her stomach and Naomi couldn't bare to open her eyes.

"Do I get the job?" Dante asked.

"Oh no... Not yet... You know its gonna be hard work..." Naomi

replied, losing her grip on his face.
Dante noticed the moment of weakness and lifted her onto the sofa before she could complain or regain control.
Her eyes were still closed and she was compliant as he lay her on her back and lifted her thigh onto his shoulder. He paused as he looked down at her.
Naomi felt his eyes on her as she snapped out of her trance.
"What you stopping for?" Naomi asked, adjusting herself to receive him.
"Just want you to look at me before you come," Dante said assuredly.
"IF I come?"
"Remember I said so, yeah?"
Before Naomi could respond, Dante lifted her other leg onto his strong shoulder. All she could do was watch, but she wanted to anyway.
Watching his hands disappear between her thighs then feeling his erection slide gracefully through her was a picture for her mind.
Naomi registered that he slipped in further than he did in the previous position.
Much further.

Dante leaned her legs over until her ankles rested either side of her head.
Her face was a picture of confusion and wonder, but Dante was past the point of caring. He knew in this position, he could make ANY woman come and Naomi was about to be no exception.
He slid his hands down to her cheeks and made his way to her pussy lips, parting them with his fingers. At the same time, he thrust deep into her and she sucked in the deepest breath.
"Whoa, whoa, whoa," Naomi sighed. "What the fuck was that?"
"What this?"
Dante did it again.
"Yeah that?"
"Did you like it Queen Naomi?"
Naomi grinned ever so sweetly, "Call me that and do THAT again."

Dante made sure his fingers held her open as he looked deep into her eyes and withdrew himself fully. As slow as he could manage, his hips fell towards her, his length filling her with each descent.
"Is that it Queen Naomi?"

"Ohhh, you NEED to keep dropping that dick on me..."

Deeper he fell into her and she was squirming and writhing beneath him.

"There's more dick to come my queen..."
"I AM a queeeeeeen..."
Before he reached her tip, he stopped.
"Thank God you stopped," Naomi said breathlessly.
"I haven't."

Dante filled her with the remaining few inches of his dick and Naomi barked loudly then stopped like it was Hammer time.
She suddenly started flapping around, like she was trying to get out of a sinking boat. Her hands reached for his face, his shoulders and her nails were out.
He held her arms down and slipped out before ramming himself back into place.
Her pussy spoke in a moist language all over Dante's dick and the sofa scooted across the floor.

"Ohhhh...noooooooooo faaaiiiiirrr..."
Naomi's hand gripped into fists and her face morphed from a smile to a devious frown.
    She knew the way her voice trailed off into silence meant that she was going to have to give him the raise on his salary.
    Her body wanted to flex and curl but she was trapped beneath him and he had her in a position where she couldn't do much but take it.

Naomi suddenly felt an electric feeling ripple through her and she flinched, continually, for a few seconds. Her whole body shuddered down to her toes and she forced him out and off her.
She rolled her thighs into a ball and hugged herself.
Dante sat back hard and proud. He still had mileage in his vehicle yet.
Naomi shivered on the other side of the sofa and gripped tight to her thighs.
Whatever he turned on inside her, it was not ready to turn off yet.

"Queen Naomi..."
Shiver.

"Queeeeeeen Naaaaoooomi?"

"Stop it!" She stuttered.

"Can't turn it off can you?"

"Fuck..." She started, but he was right. She couldn't turn it off.

"...You..."

Her face was obscured by her hair but Dante could see her lips sucking in precious air as her sides contracted.

"I think you just did."

Naomi sat in her protective ball for what felt like an eternity. Her legs were stuck in her chest and her shoulders ached as she tried to control the constant orgasm that Dante set off in her midsection.

She looked up to see Dante sitting across from her, dick still up and in full working order.

The shakes in her stomach and thighs subdued but still made her shiver.

"What..." Naomi began, grabbing at the sofa to lift herself upright. "... the fuck was that?"

"I told you didn't I? I told you you would come in that position?"

"Yeah, you did but, what the FUCK was that?" Naomi was dumbfounded.

"That, Queen Naomi, was what they call a multiple orgasm."

"FAAACK ORF! I've had multiple orgasms before and they've NEVER felt like THAT."

"Then you've never had a multiple orgasm before," Dante said, stroking his erection.

"Well played. You win. Salary raise. Shit, might have to get you a company car too."

Breathing to a rhythm, Naomi mustered enough energy to reach Dante and sit across his lap, with his dick resting against her breast.

"So," Naomi started. "You want the job?"

"Yeah, I think I could do this job pretty well." Dante whispered.

"Good, welcome to the team."

And then she climbed up off him and made her way, shakily, to her chair.

She ducked down behind her desk and rose with her bra sliding round from back to front. She ducked again and rose with her work shirt on, buttoned halfway to the top.

Dante sat up at this point.

"Erm..." He choked as Naomi got dressed in front of him. Before he found his voice, she slipped into her heels and was packing her handbag.

"Erm, Naomi? I thought we were..."

She looked up from her handbag, "We WERE... But you won the game right? So we're NOT anymore."

Dante frowned, "But I didn't get to come though, that's kinda selfish, wouldn't you say?"

Naomi walked over to Dante and sat across from him with her thighs open. "Not so much AL DANTE, and I'll tell you why..."

Oh shit, Dante thought.

He knew that when Naomi said she wanted to play a game, he felt cautious about saying yes to her. And with good reason too as the punchline to the joke was about to be delivered.

"The aim of the game was for you to get turned on enough to make ME come, correct?"

"Yeah?" Dante replied nervously.

"Did you make me come Dante?"

"Yeaaaah?"

"So you won the game. You get a salary upgrade before you start work and a company car."

"Oh, a car? Nah, hold on, what about my orgasm?" Dante asked, watching his erection wilt.

"Oh, that's for another game."

WHAT? Dante thought to himself.

Naomi stroked his face, fiddled with his limp dick and collected her stuff.

"Are you REALLY about to leave me here like..."

Naomi's phone interrupted him and she went searching through her giant handbag.

She found and answered it.

"Yes gyal, I'm leaving work now... Uh huh... What? Of course I did... Had me doing some fish flopping business... Hold on..."

Naomi turned to Dante as she reached her office door. She didn't mean to laugh at his stoic face but he looked distraught.

"Dante, welcome to the team, its gonna be a pleasure to have

you and, I'll see you Monday..."
Naomi blew him a kiss, gave him peace fingers and was gone.

"He was amazing. What... Of course I gave him the job... Not that job you dutty gal, I'm not you. I bet you gave that nurse guy of yours head already innit?"
And with that, Naomi left the building as her voice was enveloped by the descending lift.

Dante sat bollock naked, except for his socks, on Naomi's sofa. He looked at the lift and watched it reach the ground floor. That's when he realised that Naomi had actually left the building and was not coming back.
"She's actually left man here with my dick all hard and no nut? I think I've just had the piss taken out of me!"

Escaping Temptation

Stefan

A chocolate man, standing at a solid six foot three, was elbow deep in wires and cables under a makeshift desk, which was really an old door. He attempted to wrap them neatly in his space as he scanned the five security screens he set up in his cubby hole. One camera on the front door, one on the back door, two on the meeting spot and one dark screen.
He planned to arrive more than two hours before the meeting to set-up his cameras but today was not going according to plan. But it wasn't his fault... the spanner in his machine wasn't a what... but a who.
And this was not how he worked.

Well known in the criminal underworld of London town, Stefan was not only imposing as an enforcer but he excelled when it came to surveillance and plotting routes of escape out of tight situations. It was what he did. That was what the boss hired him for.
Any job he put his name on went like clockwork and he was proud of this perfect record that many gangsters could not obtain.
Because they were gangsters! Or at least tried to be. And gangsters were stupid as they were always blinded by their greed and need for acceptance and expansion, which always fucked them up in the end.

But it wasn't his fault that he was late, thus not able to set up all the microphones he wanted to plant in the bar, nor the thermal imaging monitor, which was always standard. This meant that anyone could walk in with a neatly hidden weapon that could fuck up EVERYTHING!
And by everything, Stefan wasn't thinking about the deal that was set to go down in Birds Of Paradise Bar, his mind was elsewhere.

Scanning the four working screens in front of him, happy with the space he'd created in his hole, Stefan sat back and exhaled. He stared at the ceiling and wondered if he was doing the right thing.
"You know, when you exhale, you sound like you're eating a piece of fruit that is sweeter than you thought it would be."

Her voice.
In his head.
Rattling around like a pinball, knocking against his wants, bashing against his baser animal instincts, slamming along his rationale.

Not good for business, he thought as her words made his stomach tingle.

He stared at each screen, watching for players in the game to appear but he had another 15 minutes before he EXPECTED anyone to arrive. Thinking like the criminals he worked for, he knew the OTHER SIDE would send their own 'computer whiz' to get to the venue early and scan it over for any potential danger issues. But Stefan was smoother than that and found the perfect spot to set up; an old cloak room with a door that looked like a part of the bar's exterior walls.
Their 'whiz' would never find it.

He ran a strong hand over his head, fiddled with the tracking on one of the camera screens and tried to ignore the voice that was still dancing in his subconscious.
Stefan wanted more than anything to allow the voice to two-step with his thoughts but he, of all people, knew how fucked up his professional life would become if he let his guard down.
That didn't make it any harder for Koko, the boss's girlfriend, to sell him a dream of leaving his life of working for others behind and make a new life with her.

Bang on her sales pitch which managed to connect with the lack of enjoyment he was feeling about his position in life.
Not that he wasn't happy... the amount of money he was making, there was no way he couldn't at least raise a smile. But, personally, he wasn't happy to make that money working with the type of people he did.
But leave it all?

His Pharrell Williams Dim The Lights ringtone sounded softly and he shook his train of thought and looked at the screen.
A question mark was ringing him.
He knew who it was without flinching, though he stared at the screen before answering.
Stefan sighed. "You can't keep calling me you know?"
"Why, scared I'll say something you like?"
"You already have."

"Well before we start singing Midnight Train To Georgia, you need to make sure your shit is ready 'cuz we're leaving now. Is EVERYTHING ready?"

Everything. EVERYTHING.
If Koko meant had he packed his life away into one duffel bag and stored it, then yes, he had everything ready.

"I've BEEN ready..."
"We'll see..." Koko whispered.
Stefan could hear HIS voice in the background before she hung up.

He was ready!

So ready that he flicked through his BlackBerry and watched the video he made while Koko gave him what can only be described as 'heavenly' head.
And in the boss's bed.

Koko

Sitting in the back of the limo, Koko sat nervously thinking over the plan.
Walter and his briefcase plopped beside her. He snorted phlegm down his throat and immediately opened the locket around his neck. He scooped angel dust with his baby finger nail, drawing the stardust up his huge nostril.
The same again with the other nostril.

Scoop, fly.
He rubbed the remaining residue on his gums.

"Hey baby, loosen up," Walter said, tipping some onto the corner of his credit card.
She put her tiny nostril to the card, with Walter watching her through glazed eyes as the dust vanished.
She took a long pull on her cigarette, flicking the ash out the window as they pull off.
Answering his phone with one hand, Walter slid his other hand between her legs, slipping his fingers up to her pussy.
Up close and personal, he kissed her neck and she tensed up.
"Stop please stop, STOP IT!" she shouts pushing him away.
Pissed at the rejection, he raised his fist, lining it with her jaw line without breaking his conversation. She flinches, lifting her hand to

protect her face.

"I'd smack your face off if you didn't cost me so much with the brothers," he said running his tongue up the side of her face. "You know your my best skeezer, that's why your mine."

He forced his hand inside her crotch; caressing the walls of her love but she said nothing just silent tears rolling down her face. She chanted in her head:

"Just two more hours, just two more hours, just two more hours..."

Thirty minutes later, Koko strolled into the temple of fornication, lust and desires with Walter leading her way. Before they properly entered the busy bar, people approached Walter in respect of his arrival.

"Wah gwan bless, you cool?" Was Walter's chant for the first ten minutes.

A lady with skin the shade of honey and the figure of an hourglass greeted them.

"Good evening Walter."

"What's hanging Rachel?" he said, handing her his tailor-made coat.

"I'm sure you'll show me later."

Koko shoves her coat into the hostess hand thinking to herself, 'Fucking tart! The bitch doesn't even hide the fact she fucked Walter in MY bathtub today.'

"Get us two bottles of Cristal," Koko demanded.

"You best believe I'll show you what's hanging," Walter taunted, slapping Rachel on her apple bottom.

Koko walked off to the VIP seating area with Curtis Mayfield's Pusherman putting a swing in her step. There was something powerful about being a top gangster's girlfriend; it was a far cry from being pushed about when she was a nobody stripping for a tenner in Soho.

Placing her well-toned back spring on the cushy sofa, she watched people getting in the mood; flirting, touching, drinking, negotiating, snorting, drug taking and other recommended potions in motion. Weed smoke clung to the air like fog on a field but Koko's attention was on the cameras.

She caught a glimpse of a camera neatly tucked away in the corner of the bar. She kissed her index finger and blew a kiss to the camera, knowing Stefan was watching.

After a few minutes, four gentlemen walked in tandem to their table. Eric, Ryan, Trevor and Dizzy, the other side's 'computer whiz'.

Koko greeted them all with half nods before excusing herself as she always does when Walter is doing business.

That was always the time to go 'powder' her nose.

She sauntered past dancing patrons on her way to the toilet, when she walked past an open door. Sniffing hard, she could see a room with men and women crowded in a circle, paying attention to something in front of them and sex in the air.
"Excuse me gentlemen," she said to a group of tall men watching.

They looked her up and down with hunger painted across their faces.

They parted like the Red Sea and she stepped between them. She could see them fighting the urge to touch her but she could see the respect in their demeanour.

They knew she was untouchable.

Etching her way to the front of the group, a waitress placed a flute of champagne in her well-manicured fingers.

Three women were on the floor before her; a thick woman with short, cropped hair and caramel skin was wearing a strap-on and had a second woman's legs wrapped round her body riding it like a tide. Koko couldn't make out the rest of her face because a third woman was sitting on it bouncing her ass on her waiting tongue, moaning tunes to a rhythm with the lyrics screaming, 'I'm about to cum'.

Koko was mesmerised.

Watching such freedom in front of her very eyes made her think of the freedom she would soon share with Stefan.

Searching for a camera, she took in the room and realised a ritual had begun. Men and women and women and women were touching each other, caressing, kissing, wanking and fucking. The ones that weren't doing anything were watching in amazement, there was something sexy about watching people fuck without a thought or care who was watching. And that was what kept Koko in place.

The performance turned her on so much, she could feel her panties starting to soak and cool against her warmth.
Satisfied with the eye-gasm, and planning to return, she took off towards the women's toilet, still enjoying the looks she wasn't

getting and the reasons why. She stopped in front of the toilet door to finish her drink and smooth down her Gucci dress when a hand snatched her from a hole in the wall into what looked like an old cloakroom.

"So THIS is where you been hiding, eh?"

She looked Stefan up and down like a massive piece of chocolate, licking her lips. Her breathing became heavy as she took in every inch of her 'sex god'.

Stefan

"I got the kiss you sent me," he said, feeling Koko's breath suck out of her as she nestled between his arms.

"I knew you were watching."

Koko's smile was Stefan's weakness as she kissed him with electricity and energy surging between them. He could feel her nervousness at being mere feet away from a man who would kill her if he could see through walls. And Stefan knew he'd be taking an earth nap on a building site somewhere in the foundations of the Olympic Village if this didn't go to plan.

Koko managed to jump into his grasp and wrap her thighs behind him, their kiss unbroken. Her body was excited to be around him and his erection told her the feeling was reciprocal.

With Koko attached to his lips, Stefan tried to talk, "Listen babe... we need to do this just right, otherwise, we're ALL fucked, ya understand?"

Unhitching her from his torso like a Velcro vixen, Stefan held her against his station of active monitors and looked into her eyes.

"Koko, I'm serious. You know what he's like when it comes to things like his DVDs so what do you think is gonna happen when he pieces this together?"

Fighting against his strong grip, Koko's heart was beating and she wriggled loose, allowing her hands to run up and down his, always warm, body.

"You think I care? Fuck him, fuck Eric, fuck Ryan, DEFINATELY fuck Trevor, ugly piece of shit. And fuck Dizzy... cock-eyed fucker! I don't care about anything else right now except for what's in this room... do you know what I just saw right outside..."

"KOKO? This is serious... this ain't no joke suttin', this is our lives here. We both know how trigger happy Trevor is... he wouldn't blink before shooting us both."

"Does that turn you on? The fact that you could die?" Koko

asked, her hands playing with his zip.

"Death doesn't REALLY do it for me you know. I'm more a fan of breathing normally, a big booty and living healthily."

Koko was lost in her fingers working his zip without him noticing. Her hand was trailing the inside of his trousers before he could react and she released his semi.

Her face was made up with deviousness; sneaky shadowing her eyes and cunning making her lips shine in his cubby hole.

If time wasn't so tight, Stefan would easily allow Koko to engage him. Use her hand to start working the length of his shaft, using his sticky pre-cum to slide more easily. Take him out of his trousers and drop to her knees in front of him.

With Walter sipping a Stella while feeling Rachel's available backside on his third monitor, Stefan looked down to see Koko folding him into her mouth.

"Koko, no... we don't have..."

Stefan knew it was too late. Lost in the thoughts of what she could be doing, he wasn't watching what she was actually doing and she caught him slipping. So she slipped him in.

Her lips pursed in front of his head, she slid him in slowly, pushing him through her closed mouth. She stopped mid-shaft and looked up at Stefan, who always loved to watch. Their eyes spoke as Walter huddled with his boys and cock-eyed Dizzy disappeared out of frame. Stefan wanted to follow him across the screens but Koko demanded his attention.

Her eyes and lips were soft and Stefan was a picture of control, but her eyes always did something to him. Soft, honey brown and asking him a question.

'Can I have it all?'

His deep, brandy brown eyes wanted to answer but time was not their friend and he could feel 'beef' rising in the air. But, with Koko, he felt like time could wait.

'You can have anything you want.'

Koko slipped her handbag off her shoulder, released her mouth, opened wide and took Stefan until her lips reached his stomach. She held her mouth open, flexing her throat against his length, saliva creating a slapping sound.

"Anything you want..." Stefan said, closing his eyes to the images

of the club that beamed behind Koko's kneeling frame.
She hummed on his dick and watched him react with a giggle, a sound that always made her feel good inside.
In the background, Stefan's black monitor came to life. The sudden change in light made him open his eyes, dragging himself from the ecstasy of Koko's warm mouth.
Reaching over to adjust the zoom, he saw a group of half naked people surrounding a...
"What the hell is this?" Stefan said, his body trembling from good head but his mind clouded with fear.
His escape room... the way out of this whole thing... his ace in the hole, was now compromised and he had no idea who the people were or where they came from. He just knew that his whole plan was fucked.
He raised the volume on the camera in the room and he could decipher three separate moans coming from the room. But he couldn't see what everyone was looking at.
Sliding his dick into her cheek, Koko turned to the screen and moaned. "That's the room I was trying to tell you about. There's some SHIT going on in there. Actually, leave the volume up."
Stefan didn't know what to say. He didn't know how to tell Koko that his big plan was fucked by the fact that people were... fucking.
His brow was now drenched and his heart was beating so fast, he could feel it in his throat. He had no time to think as Koko made his dick a sloppy mess in her grasp.
Watching her work, the way she slid saliva onto his dick and sucked it back into her mouth, was ALWAYS a mistake, but he always looked.
"Baby... look... oh shiiiiiiit.... babe... I've gotta... gotta..."
   Stefan stopped speaking as his hips spoke for him and thrust his wet dick into Koko's open mouth, with her tongue out. He held her head steady and circled his hips.
Walter's sudden movement on the monitor drew his attention. His boss was now drawing a weapon and running out of the camera's sight.
"Oh shit... babe..."
Stefan looked down again and met Koko's dreamy brown eyes and felt his body warming up and a cold shiver running down his back.
Gunshots rang out in the club and Stefan's camera screens were a scurry of activity, people running towards exits, random shooters

popping off and Walter disappearing and reappearing on every screen.
His last movements were caught on one screen and Walter had his gun cocked, walking in their general direction.
Koko didn't flinch. "You better come in my mouth."

Koko

Koko realised she was losing Stefan's attention to the commotion that was going on behind her on the monitors. She heard three loud shots which startled her, almost making her jam her teeth into the flesh between her lips.
Stefan snatched his piece from her mouth; he was concentrating on the screens before him. Koko watched his dick dry before her eyes.
She stood up, turned his face to hers and kissed him passionately, forcing her tongue in his mouth.
One kiss was all it took to make him forget about Walter running around Bird's Of Paradise Bar with his favourite gun out, ready to shoot anyone who stood in his way.

Koko's heart beat for Stefan, for the two of them.
They shared a forbidden love they tried so hard to avoid, for they toyed with death. But in the end it didn't stop Stefan pulling Koko into his strong arms, sharing deep passionate kisses.
His finger's wandered into Koko's knickers and, with the madness going on in the bar drifting away, brought back memories of when she first met him.

    She was lying in the sun on a lounger by the pool reading a book, his delicious cologne arrived before he did. She looked up to see a delectable specimen of a man standing before her. The fire in her belly was instant.
    She would daydream about him doing the same thing; putting a fire in her belly. Just to put his hands in her knickers and play with her, to have those long fingers caress her walls when Walter was drunk by the pool. He always managed to bring back the same feelings of lust that made her weak every time, there was no one who would tell her otherwise.
All those times when Stefan would come to 'check up' on her when Walter was away on business trips were spent exploring the heights of sexual creativity in his eight-bedroom mansion in

Hertfordshire.

In Koko's mind, body and soul, they had a future to be erected, but first they had a past to escape.

Koko's hands wandered back to Stefan's piece, not once taking any notice of the gunshots ringing around her. In his presence she felt safe and knew that he had a plan to get them out of there. She played with his sticky pre-cum and welcomed his hardness, his fingers inside her walls and his tongue on her teeth.
Pulling his buttons off his tailored shirt, she ran her hands under his vest and over his corrugated stomach.
He unzipped her dress peeling her out like a banana; revealing her plump breasts and beautiful skin, watching it drop to the floor.
Koko sighed at his charisma, his talent to make her forget to breathe.
He pulled her lace panties down, careful not to tangle them in her heels.
She stood in front of him like a perfect painting.
Glistening beads of sweat ran down her back in the dimly lit furnace of a cloak room. Wearing nothing but Prada heels and a diamond choker, to cover the bruises Walter put around her neck, Koko stepped into Stefan's breathing space. He picked her up with ease and placed her on the desk, parting her legs wide and high.

Staring into her eyes, he dropped to one knee in front of her pursed her lips with his tongue, the sensation making her hold her breath.

She felt his warm wet tongue dive in to her opening.

Letting out a moan, she pushed her hips into his chin, holding his head as she fucked his tongue.
Stefan knew how to heal her from the inside and make all her anxieties go away, calming her instantly.

Grinding her hips frantically, her moans ringing in his ears, the gun shots popping in the distance, all combined but didn't faze either of them.
Her moans told him she was going to burst her juices on his face but he kept sucking her swollen clit, her favourite sensation. She played with her nipples sucking them; encircling her tongue on the left one, the right one, both.
Her pussy contracted, letting a warm liquid coat Stefan's mouth. The show made his dick harder.

He stood up while licking his lips, pulled her toward him and kissed her, letting the essence of her smother their kiss.
Koko pushed him back until he hit the chair with his leg. He was forced into the seat before he could make the decision and she straddled him, with perfect aim. Letting him into her wetness, she began to ride him, waiting for him to throw his head back as he always did.
Gunshots still popping off, deafening screams, but it was Koko and Stefan's world.
Koko kept riding him, sending him into a trance. The sensation oh so good, so good.
He stood up making her stand with him and turned her round, making her touch the ground.
A rude intrusion but mind blowing sensation inside her pussy and goosebumps frazzled her body, sending her into outer space with her mind in another dimension.

He stroked her, stirred her coffee. She tried to stand, but he forced her head down to her knees, bringing her perfect peach into his dick while his balls beat against clit. He found his favourite spot inside her and made himself at home.
Koko bit her bottom lip, she could almost taste the blood filling its plump pinkness.

Stefan

With no warning, three loud shots popped off and Stefan looked at the screens to see Walter kicking and bussing shots at the door to their cubby hole.

Koko was completely bent over and couldn't see what the silent screen was showing but he could hear the impact of the bullets sucking into the wall of bulletproof vests he attached to the door upon his arrival.
Without panicking, Stefan moved quickly. He knew the door wouldn't hold for long but long enough to get done what he needed to do.
Koko began to alternate the flick of her cheeks, making sure he was as deep as he could go. Holding onto her ankles, Koko pounded on his dick, while he tried to reach into the pocket of his trousers which were bunched around his ankles. Koko was pounding him, using the table above her to catch herself and rock backwards and forwards into him.

Pressing a small pen in his pocket, two panels from the ceiling separated and two thick wires dropped to the floor.

Frantically, Stefan tried to focus away from Koko's apple shape and the moistness that was dripping off his testicles and hook her up. Attempting to attach one of the wires around Koko's moving waist, Stefan kept an eye on the door of vests, which was wobbling.

"Kinky time now?" Koko asked from below.

With his dick hard, wet and getting wetter, Stefan attached Koko's wire around her waist securely then hooked his.
"OPEN THE FUCKING DOOR... I KNOW YOU'RE IN THERE... MY GUN KNOWS YOU'RE IN THERE WITH MY BITCH..."
"Is that Walter?" Koko said, trying to stand upright.
"Shhh..." Stefan returned, drawing his trousers up, but leaving his zip down. He slung his rucksack over his back and took ONE safety check on everything before he turned off the lights. Working the controls in the dark, with Koko's sugar walls flexing, he zoomed in on the screen showing Walter at a medium close up.

"Hey Walter?" Stefan said, watching his boss react to his voice.
"You know you're a fucking dead man don't you? You DO know that?"
"I'd rather live with this..."

And with that, Stefan held Koko's waist tight and slowly worked his dick in and out of her until she built up to a steady moan that he knew Walter would hear. He bent his legs so he entered from below while spreading her cheeks with one hand and spanking her with the other.

"Stef... an... who... whoo... whooo..."

Koko was now leaning on the table, grinding on him in the dark while Walter continued to lick shots at the door.
Reaching under her body, Stefan used two fingers to letterbox her clit and she shuddered instantly, letting out a guttural moan that built to the tip of her voice.
"Now that, BOSS, is how you make YOUR woman come."

Stefan knew that would more than infuriate Walter and his action promoted his boss's reaction as he disappeared from the screen and reappeared holding an AR-15 assault weapon at the door.
But more importantly than the military-issued assault rifle he was

holding was the fact that, for the first time today, Walter wasn't holding his precious briefcase.

Exactly what Stefan hoped for.

"SHIT," Stefan said as he reached for this pocket again. "Hold on baby... hold that position."

Wrapping his arms around Koko's vibrating waist, and thrusting himself deep enough to stay inside her, Stefan clicked the tip of the pen. The wires suddenly retracted and slowly pulled them off the ground and through the open panels and into a pitch black vent.

Koko, who viewed the whole thing while holding her ankles, watched the ceiling panels close behind them as they jerked to a sudden stop.

Silence.
New darkness.

Koko could feel her legs dangling but couldn't see them in the black before her eyes. The vent was musty and she could hear the scuttling of feet all around her. But Stefan's strong arm around her waist told her she was fine.

She felt for a steady surface to walk her hands up in order to hang upright.

"What the fuck just..."

"Shh... watch this..."

Stefan showed Koko a night-vision video feed of the room they just disappeared from. On the screen, the door burst open and Walter, gun in one hand and briefcase in the other, stumbled into the dark room with his weapon trained on everything.

Walter felt a path with his legs, intent on not getting caught slipping by one of the best tricksters in the gangster game.

Anything he knocked into came face-to-face with the muzzle of the rifle and Stefan enjoyed watching him stumble in the darkness. All his gangster power, his strength, his command of life and death, stripped away and left a small boy with a big gun stumbling in the dark.

Above him, Stefan counted down in his head from 60, while Koko turned to face him, awakening his dangling dick with her moist grip.

Building a slow rhythm, with the swing of the wires, Stefan wrapped Koko's legs around his waist. As easy as his erection slipped into her, it felt like he was meant to be there.

"48... 47... 46... 45...44..." Stefan counted, using the light from the video screen to illuminate Koko's face.

"Why you counting?"

"...42... You'll see... 40..."

"So I've got time to do this then?"

Koko wrapped her arms around his shoulders and lifted herself up and down on him. He was submerged in her pillow soft insides and with her Gucci dress bunched around her waist, she used her exposed pussy as a lubricant and worked around the wires that suspended them.

Stefan closed his eyes as Walter prowled in the darkness, using his gun to feel out the room. Stumbling on a chair, Stefan figured out where Walter was in the room.

Koko was now holding his mini-LED screen so he could see the room and used the light to shine on his face as he struggled to count.

"...33...32...3...1..."

"By the time you get to 15, I'm gonna come..."

With their eyes locked, and Walter stumbling below, Koko exhaled as Stefan inhaled, riding against the sway of their bodies.

Her feet stretched behind him and found the back of the vent, giving her some leverage.

They didn't share any kisses, they just stared at each other, their faces daring the other to flinch.

"... 26... 25... 5... 24... 23... 3... 3... oh 3..."

Koko was thumping her hips on his dick and her circular movement took his focus momentarily. And in all his years doing what he did, this was a first.

Stefan grinned. "... 22... 21...20..."

"Keep counting baby..." Koko whispered.

CRASH...

Stefan kept his eyes firmly on Koko, watching her lips fight to stay closed and not let out the scream she was dying to release. He didn't care what Walter crashed into underneath because, in a few more seconds, it was all going to be over.

"... 19... 18..."

Her hand popping his erection in and out of her quickly was the right note for her song as Stefan watched her struggle to stay silent.

"Shhh... 17... 16..."

"I... I can't... can't... oh... oh... ohhh... STEF..."

Stefan froze. "Oh shit..."

As she built to her crescendo, Stefan immediately looked at the screen expecting the worst. And the worst is what stared back at him.

Walter was looking up at the panels above him and was in the process of swinging the gun towards the ceiling, in their direction, while Koko was bucking against him.

"...FAN ... I'm coming..." she finished shouting.

"Shit... Hold on..."

Wrapping his arms around her again, Stefan released the pulley system with the click of the pen and the pair of them fell straight through the ceiling panels, bringing four surrounding panels crashing down with them.

With a whole heap of noise, Stefan broke through first with his feet and was able to kick the barrel of the gun away from their direction as they dropped.

Stefan's other foot landed a crunching kick in Walter's face and, though it happened so quickly, he was sure he heard and felt something crack.

Trying to stick the landing, while holding Koko was harder than Stefan thought and he managed to semi-land on his feet. He slipped on the cables he fought so hard to put away earlier and fell backwards with Koko on top of him onto the crumpled Walter, who was motionless beneath them.

Stefan twisted his ankle on the way down and knew it was more than a sprain, but he knew his feet were the least of his worries. Least he managed to score two good kicks.

Koko was sucking air through her teeth as she let out a low moan that sounded like pleasure and pain.

"You ok? You should be, you landed on me."

"Wasn't that the plan?" Koko replied.

"Not really..."

Stefan hobbled up and pulled Koko to her feet before she was ready. She swayed on her feet, expecting her stilettos to help support her but her heels were lost in the madness.

"Looking for these?"

While wrestling the briefcase from Walter's quiet carcass, Stefan drew Koko's attention to her heels which were embedded in his ex-boss's temple. His bloody face was slumped to the side and yet he still managed to sport that 'fuck you' grin.

"Is he..."

"Do you wanna find out or do you wanna get out of here and fly?" Stefan asked, dusting her down and straightening her diamond choker.
"Let's fly... fly every time..."

Stefan looked back at the fallen, possibly deceased, Walter. As he held Koko in his arms and manoeuvred them between the hole they made, he smiled.
"Ready baby?"

Looking down at Walter, who was literally wearing her heels with a smile, brought a sense of relief over Koko as she looked back to Stefan.
    She spat on the quiet Walter and sighed heavily.
"I had the best orgasm you know," she said, running her hands over his face.
"Sorry I missed it... maybe we can take the wires with us and try again somewhere else," Stefan replied and pressed the button in his pocket.

    Quicker than before, the pair of them were sucked back into the vent by their waists and up towards the roof, where Stefan had his cousin Royston, who was a full-fledged helicopter pilot, on standby.
The sound of the air passing by them made them feel like they were flying. Koko hugged him and held onto his body as tight as she could.
    They did not plan to let each other go.

Ladies Nite

CHARLOTTE

The room was warm and clean.
A faint smell of curry goat and coconut cream tainted the air. I watched as the sun seeped through the open curtain, bounce across the room and reflect back on its self through the mirror on the far side.

As I glanced around the room, feeling proud of how well I kept it, my eyes settled on the two chairs that sat so sturdily in the middle. The one I always sit on was ruffled a little, the cushion impressed from where I would always lean to change the channel or reach for my glass of wine. The empty chair opposite was neat and tidy.

Still fixated on the two chairs, I remembered how he used to throw me down and slowly pull my thong off with his teeth and spread my legs wide across the sofa, one foot on each arm. He used to like me to watch as he put the tip of his tongue on my clit and grabbed my hips as my back arched with the thrill of his soft tongue on my rock hard button. He used to like the way I moved my hips as he worked me into a violent frenzy.

I remember how he used to tear my clothes off and throw them across the room in desperation to fuck me.
I remember how he used to long to reach home just so he could kiss my face and feel my eye lashes tickle his cheek.
I remember how he used to hold me.
I remember how beautiful he thought I was, naked in the candle light.
I remember how he used to want me.
I remember how he used to love me.

I snapped out of my daydream and slowly came back to the reality of the empty room. It was picture perfect in every way, like something out of Style Magazine, but all of a sudden there was an icy breeze that seemed to flow through it.
The sunlight didn't seem so bright, the aroma of curry and coconut had gone stale and the room seemed to be more empty than tidy.

I walked across the freshly varnished floors and the echo of my heels made the room feel even emptier. I stepped in front of the mirror for a final check. The midnight blue dress was a perfect choice. It hugged my hips, flowed perfectly over my breasts and accentuated the roundness of my arse.

If he didn't want me, another man would.

I had waited for him. Waited and waited, we were living separate lives. I finally opened my eyes.

It was almost time to leave, the prospect of a family function would usually fill me with dread, but there was something different about the air tonight.
I felt strong.
I felt wild.
I grabbed my purse and my keys. When he came home there would be no note to explain where I was. I glanced back at the room; it was a perfect metaphor for our marriage.

    I'm stepping outside the box
Erasing the lines that tend to confine
Pushing my limits
No bars
No holds
Some might say I'm walking blind
I choose to leave the loneliness behind
Seeking an open mind
Kicking inhibition aside
The old me remains sitting on the side...
Watching...
Waiting for a man who is no longer mine

    I stepped into the bar, masks all around. Uncle Franklin, or dad to me and Nadia, did say he wanted to get everyone talking and mingling outside of their normal groups. The masks had to be his crazy idea.
I smiled to hide my frown as I walked past a group of gossiping aunties, I had no physical mask. I hovered around, alone, looking for a familiar face.
I tried to spot my friend Nia or my sister Nadia. I wanted to get the pleasantries with them over.
Especially Nadia, I could just see her smug face asking me how my husband was and if I was doing anything more than being a housewife. She had never approved of me giving up my career to be Trey's wife.
She didn't understand.
She would never know how good it felt to wash and fold his

clothes or spend the whole afternoon cooking a meal and seeing the satisfaction on his face when he finished it.
Apparently she was engaged to be married, but had no idea how to be a wife.

I continued looking around to see if I could see any of my other family members. I wondered what masks they would be wearing. It felt like I was being watched, but everyone seemed occupied in their own conversations. I guess I would hang out by the bar until I found someone to have a mindless conversation with.

I leaned against one of the pillars to scan the room again, desperate for a drink, and that's when my eyes met his mask.

He was standing just in front of the bar; tall, built, strong and masculine.
A beautiful stranger.

I could see the definition of his body through his shirt; he was just what I wanted, big hands and long fingers. He was wearing a mask, but I knew he was looking directly at me. I could feel it. I felt it from the moment I entered the bar, but only just realised. I lowered my eyes, letting my lashes hide my growing desire. I had to pass him to get to the bar.
I bit my lip, switched my hips and walked by.
As I passed him he lent forward and dropped something directly in front of me. I looked down and saw it was a key. He bent down as if to pick it up and looked at me. He looked deep into me, like he knew who I was, what I needed, what I had been missing for so long. I could just about make his eyes out through the mask. They were deep and hazel.
I caught a glimpse of his skin, smooth and pecan coloured. I could feel my pussy moisten with every second spent looking at this man. I squeezed my legs together to keep my longing at bay. He twitched as if he could smell the aroma of my pussy coming alive.

I can't help it if he puts me in a daze
Feels like a loss of control
I'm not wanting to show, how this stranger makes my pussy juices flow
I can imagine his head going real low...
Nice and slow...
Give it to me deeper...

Deeper...
DEEPER...

Before I knew it I was against the wall in an empty upstairs room. He took his mask off and I saw his face for the first time. Chiselled, strong, dark, mysterious and mystifying.
He slowly peeled my dress off and let it fall to the floor, never taking his eyes off me. He pulled me close to his chest, I caught the fragrance of his cologne, I breathed it in, tasted it then exhaled. He ran his masculine hands down the length of my body carefully rolling his thumbs delicately over each curve. He made me shiver.
This was how it felt when a man gave a woman the fever. He unclipped my bra and drew it down my arms with such precision and ease.
He stood back and looked at me, really looked at me, just the way he had done in the bar. I put my hands up to hide my nakedness; he moved them away and said, "I want to look at you".

He studied me for what seemed like an eternity. As he searched me with his eyes I began to feel my emotions light up, my body awaken and my pussy overflow like the violent rainfall of an angry storm.

Still gazing at me, he began taking his shirt off. I reached out to unbuckle him and he smiled the most intoxicating smile I've ever seen, I could feel myself melt into him. I pulled his jeans down revealing his perfectly toned thighs. I let my lips pass over his package.
He was carrying big things!

I closed my eyes and imagined how good he was going to feel inside of me. A vision of Trey suddenly passed through my mind, just for a moment. Then I remembered how many times he left me lonely. The endless texts telling me he was going to be late, again. The hunger I felt lying alone in our bed every night.

I opened my eyes and the image of him disappeared.

He put his arms around me, as if he knew that I sought such closeness. I exhaled again. He stood back and looked at me then knelt down in front of me and pulled my knickers off. He picked my thigh up, lifted it high and started licking my pussy.

The feeling he gave me was like lightning cutting through a

clear sky. I couldn't help but vocalise the pleasure he was giving me, I spread my leg wider, I wanted more intensity.

He gripped my other leg, lifting me off the ground. I was open and just wanted pleasure, more pleasure. I wanted him to make me come and let go all over his face.

I looked at this man and remembered he was a stranger but, for some wet reason, it didn't matter. With every moan I released he went deeper and deeper into my pussy, intensifying the sensation, almost making me cry.

He put me down and spun me around. He made circles, he swirled, he dabbed, he made his tongue curl. He kept sucking me, he kept kissing me, he kept tongue fucking me. With each stroke he elevated my pussy and took it to a place it had never been before. I turned my head so I could watch him work me, taste me, enjoy me. His face down in my pussy made me smile. I tasted his pleasure, it was indefinable.

I watched him momentarily.

My back arched, my face turned to the wall, I exploded all over him.

My body uncontrollably danced across the wall, reaching for something unknown. I struggled to breathe, my mouth dry from gasping for air as I slowly came down from the high he had given me.

I couldn't see clearly.

He gently lowered me down and lay me on the floor.

I could see his phallic image coming towards me, powerful and strong. I had no inhibitions.

I opened my legs wide and used my fingers to open my pussy.

I wanted him to fuck me.

I was hungry.

As if he knew my thoughts he put his helmet on my clit, I leaned back and let the pleasure run up and down me. He put the tip of his dick inside me and worked it upwards, my body stiffened as he instantly stimulated my G-spot.

First time.

Rubbing and touching it, my spot was filling up and craving for more. He pushed my thighs up so my knees were by my head. I screamed as his dick hit my spot in an even more intense and sensitive place, he knew just what to do. I could barely contain myself and I hoped the family could not hear my shrieks of pleasure over the bass line of the tunes playing downstairs.

He seemed to climb deeper inside me with each thrust, caressing me from the inside out and pleasuring my pussy in a way no man ever had. I lay my head right back, my hands sprawled above my head, my legs spread as wide as my hips would allow.
I felt free, I felt wild, I felt intoxicated by this stranger who seemed to make it his business to pleasure me beyond my wildest fantasy.

Everything he did to me made me yearn for more. I could feel myself reaching breaking point, about to spill over and unleash. He was looking at me whilst he was working my pussy.
At that moment, my body seemed to take control of itself. I closed my eyes, my hips began to pulsate violently and my back rose into a mound.
My mind went blank and my body was overtaken by immense pleasure, pain, throbbing...

I opened my eyes, unsure of where I was and what had happened. After a moment, I began to take in the room as the memories of the man, señor nameless, came flooding back. I got up onto my elbows and looked around.
He was gone!

I got up on my feet in an attempt to see if he was in another part of the room, but somehow I knew he wouldn't be.
He was gone.

I looked at the room in detail for the first time since I had stepped into it. It was empty, nothing but the window that looked down onto the dance floor and a skylight. It looked empty, but it was full of memories. It was the place that marked my new beginning.
It felt warm and full of emotion.
I didn't care that I didn't know his name.
I wasn't going to try and understand why he pursued me or why he left so abruptly.
His sex had awakened my subconscious desire and I knew that I wanted more pleasure like that. Still naked, I laid back down on the floor. The sun shone from above and warmed my skin, the familiar smell of home-cooked curry goat and coconut cream oozed its way into the room from downstairs.
It was fresh. I exhaled again and smiled.

NIA

"Nia?" her mum shouts up the stairs.

"I'm in the bathroom; I'm just getting ready for work. I'll be down in a minute."

"Okay."

Nia's mum, Maria, is recovering from a stroke and has to use a wheelchair and a walking frame to get to and fro. It happened a year ago but thank God she's on the mend now.

As for her dad she doesn't know much about him, all she knows is he's a bastard. And even that's too much information.

She finishes brushing her teeth and goes downstairs to help her mum get out of the wheelchair to the settee so that she can watch TV in comfort.

"Got your remote ma?"

"Yes."

"Cup of tea?"

"Right here baby, just go."

Nia exchanges usual chit chat with her mum before she leaves. With a kiss goodbye, Nia picks up her bag, checks for keys, mobile, work report and she's ready to go.

Nia finishes talking to her last resident at the hostel where she works for vulnerable young people just before 4pm. As a support worker, her long days can be incredibly long so an early finish on a Friday is always welcome.

She loves her job but her passion is to write full time.

A few of the young men in the hostel suggest she should WRITE something for them but their tone screamed sex, which was more than slightly inappropriate.

But, as thick and caramel as Nia was, it was understandable. She looked good for her age, which remained a closely guarded secret.

Grow 10 years, get a job, some facial hair and a place of your own then DON'T come and find me, she thinks to herself regularly.

"Thank God it's Friday," she says to no in particular as she leaves work. She usually meets up with her girls and they engage in some major cackalacking, gossiping and munching.

The meet-up, for Nia, became something to look forward to every week, due to the fact that there had been no relationship with a man for a long time.

Men were out there but they were the non-committing types that preferred to 'buss and be out' before the sun rises and the juices dry.
But there WAS someone who managed to keep her topped up with what she needed but as far as commitment was concerned, that was another story with him.

He always called at 6pm on the dot, not a second before or after. But she never knew what day he was going to call.

Her phone rings and Nia smiles.
"Hello?" she says with a high-pitched inflection.
"How you doing gorgeous?" he asks back.

Nia can feel her body reacting to his voice; she knows who it is, what he's going to say and how he's going to say it and it's turning her on to wait for it.

"What you doing?"
"Just finished work, now I'm going home and then I'm meeting the girls for a drink?" What are YOU doing?"
"Just chilling before work. But I was sitting here and I suddenly had the urge to see you. To feel you... to smell you... to touch you. That's what I WANT to be doing."
"You don't even need to ask twice babe, usual time, usual place?"
"Yep, see you then."

Nia can feel her pussy starting to throb because she knows what's coming, and is in agreement with her excitement.
How is a man so cute and sexy single? He must have a woman. All she's knows is that she's having fun so fuck the questions.
A quick ride home to shower, get changed, check up on mum, then out the door.

Nia's frantically looking for a parking space; it's always heaving on a Friday night. After a few minutes she finds one and eases her car in and checks herself in the mirror before making her way.
"Here goes. Could do with some more lip gloss, MAC of course."

She walks the 10 minutes until she reaches the bar where they usually meet. Her eyes search but can't see what she's looking for. Squeezing past people, Nia knows he's there, she can feel him watching her.

She tries to move feline-like through the bar, hoping she'll be

able to find him and, eventually, she sees him. Standing at six foot tall, athletic build, not too big not too slim, just right and tight, butter pecan complexion and his hair dark and long back in a ponytail.
Having made eye contact with him, she starts to walk to the rear of the building and he follows.

Nia can feel his presence behind her; she knows what time it is and her heart is beating faster. He grabs her and pushes her up against the wall.
They like to have sex outside, the excitement of someone seeing them, watching, makes it all the more enjoyable.

"You looking for me? Well you've found me, what you got for me?" He slides open the belt on her trench coat to reveal black lace top stockings, a thong and nothing else.

I got something warm, tight & moist
Ready for your cock to hoist
She spreads her legs so he can
Push the thong aside
To reveal her soft firm behind
He bends down to taste her jewelled crown
His tongue knows how to please her
Tease her
Her pussy lips are enticing him to explore and enjoy
He inserts his fingers in
Making her moan in sin
His cock is not hiding
But fighting to get in
And take over
He kisses, licks her clit
His tongue doesn't miss
As she moves in time
Her glossed lips shaped in a smile
He can feel her wanting to come
But he's not done
He unzips himself to reveal his pride
Hard and ready to glide
And glide he does
"Oohh baby I love your cock
You fill me up what the fuck"
He holds her waist

As his cock her pussy tastes
He beats her harder
She backs it up on him
Doggy is how she wants it
Likes it
Loves it
He pulls her hair
To keep the control
Of the beast inside her
He gets in deeper
Like he's going to breed her
She arches her back
Ready to take his attack
They both like it like that
She can feel it
"Oohh shit, I'm coming..."
His come face strained
"Me too baby, do what you got to do..."
They both come in time on cue
Like sexy Latino beats
That echoes in the street
He slaps her bum
That was a sweet come
Pure sensual fun

    As they both fix themselves, they stare intensely and kiss passionately. His cock is still hard as if ready to go again and her pussy could do with another go around. Their lips are not smiling, just waiting for the other person to ring the bell for round two. That is until he speaks.

    "I gotta go," he touches her face tenderly and kisses her again.

"I know babe, we'll book round two another time."

She would love to tell him 'come home with me', but she can't with her mum at home. She sighs as he kisses her forehead then walks away with the swagger of a man that just handled his business.

    Checking her vibrating phone, that has been harassing her jacket pocket for ages, Nia sees she has 20 missed calls from Nadia and Charlotte.

    Adding her destination to the Google Maps app on her phone, she finds that her meeting place with the girls is not far

away from where she stood.
Nia started walking, feeling the tickling flow of the breeze under her coat.

As she walks round to the bar entrance, she detours to the bathroom; slips on her little black dress from her handbag, checks for smeared gloss, bite marks, finger marks or cum stains before meeting her 'gal pals for life', who were still ringing off her phone.
She crossed the heaving room of masks, brushing past people with her nipples still tingling.
Then she found her girls.

"Hi sexy people," Nia says with an air of excitement, and a touch of orgasm.
"Where you been?" Charlotte asks.
"We been ringing your phone for time," Nadia added.
"Sorry, you know how it is when I'm driving."
"You need to get a handsfree girl, how long have I been saying that?" Charlotte added, handing Nia a drink.
"And how long have I been ignoring you?" Nia said with a huge sigh. "So what's going on, what's with all the masks and ting?"
The sisters filled her in on the party theme but Nia doesn't mention the previous encounter.
She never has.
It's her little secret and her own business.
The air feels free under her dress and trench coat as the old school soul music screams through the bar and everyone sings along.

'I FOUND LOVING... SINCE I FOUND YOOOOOU, I'M IN LOVE WITH YOOOOOU'.

The bar is throbbing with masked people dancing in unison.
Nia raised her drink high with everyone in the bar as she sang off-key. To her, these were the songs that make you want to make love and have sex all night long and make babies to.
Randomly, she saw someone cutting through the crowd that resembled him... similar build...
He had gone from her line of sight as she sang to Nadia and Charlotte, her zest for life refreshed.
Nia can't wait for the next time.

NADIA

"You make me so fucking hard; I want to fuck your ass so badly."

You fucking what?

I made to turn round and face the fool who had spoken to me in such a disgusting manner. But he pushed up against my back; his body touching mine so I was trapped between him and the table in my seat.

Whoever this guy was chose a lucky moment because Nia and Charlotte would've berated him to within an inch of his life. But they were on a toilet break.

I was furious but could not help but notice the large hard flesh pressed against the small of my back. The most confusing and annoying thing was the betraying tingle from my pussy in response.

What a fucking betrayal. If my body was not part of me, I would cut it off and send it into exile for its reaction to the crude words by this man.

"I've been watching you sitting here on your own," he continued. "Talking on the phone and being anti-social. But you know what? You fucking turn me rock hard, can you feel my cock against you? Can you feel it inviting you to take it in your mouth and make it sloppy and wet?"

I shook my head trying to dismiss the images being conjured up by his words, his accent intoxicating and weaving a spell around me that made me yearn to open my pussy lips and let him glide deep inside me.

What the hell am I thinking?

"Who the fuck are you?" I manage to get out through gritted teeth, not wanting to draw attention to us.

The real question though was why was I getting turned on by his words?

Why was the image of me on my knees taking his cock deep down my throat making me cream in my chair and refusing to be dislodged from my mind?

He leaned over and picked up my phone which started vibrating from an incoming call. His arm coming into view gave me a preview of what he looked like.

Firm muscular pecan-coloured arms, with a splattering of long dark hair, that sent images of a pecan cock surrounded by a matt of dark curls made me close my eyes and try to focus but all it did was intensify my other senses. He smelled of sex; a heady mix of hot fucking and a vanilla-based aftershave. The images started playing havoc in my mind.

"Who's Justin?" he asked, warm air from his lips caressing my ear as he picked up the phone so I could see the name flashing on the screen.

Oh my God, Justin!

I dug deep to find the energy to respond, missing the call accidentally.
"He is my fiancé." I said proudly, feeling the urge to flash my engagement ring at him.
"Really?"
"Yes, so you better move away from me... now!"
My breathing seemed to be escalating with each word I spoke as his hand brushed against the side of my breast. That may have had something to do with it or maybe it was the continued pressure from his cock against my back. I don't know but I may need a doctor soon because my temperature is definitely rising and for some reason I am frozen to the spot.

He chuckled; it was a deep and sexy sound that made my toes curl and my knees weaken, if I'd been standing I would have definitely stumbled.
"If you wanted me to move Nadia, you would have asked me to a long time ago. I have heard all about you and your successful businesses, luxury cars and your token trophy fiancé. You're the gold star of this family."
"I've worked hard for all I have." I replied, feeling attacked for my success.

Yes a little defensive, because I was tired of being judged for the decisions I've made. So what if this family reunion was the first time I had seen most of my extended family in four years? I was busy.
"I know you have baby, but what I want to know is; does Justin fuck you good? Does he make your toes curl and have you scream his name out loud when he licks your pussy lips?"
"Don't be disgusting," I flinched in response. He was quite crude for someone who didn't know me but, in my heart and my pussy, I

just didn't care.

"Oh, have you never had your pussy licked Nadia? Never felt the soothing pressure of a tongue as it brushes against your clit? Do you want me to fuck you with my tongue Nadia? I want you to sit on my face while I tongue fuck you and you squirt all over my face. I want to lap up every single bit of your juices as it flows onto my tongue and makes you shudder with the force of your orgasm."

"Stoooop it." I shouted without turning around to look at him.
"You KNOW you don't want me to stop. From my point of perception you want me to lift that pretty pink skirt you're wearing that shows off the beautiful roundness of your voluptuous ass and you want me to fuck you hard and fast against this wall behind us, especially with all these people in this room."

"You don't know what you are talking about."

Oh, but he did.

I was desperate to get him to stop spinning this erotic web that was making me want everything he was describing. I looked down at my phone which was vibrating again.

"Your pussy is so wet right now Nadia, let me taste you?"
"No, I told you I'm engaged."
"Is that no I CAN'T taste you or NO, your pussy isn't wet right now?
"

"Both" I replied calling his bluff and lying at the same time.

He moved away and I felt like a crack addict going cold turkey, disappointed in the fact he decided to leave the space behind me cold. The feel of his cock on my back had been comforting and his words had woven a spell that made me forget that I was in a public place surrounded over 60 members of my extended family.

"Dance with me."
He was beside me, taking my hand, trying to interlock my fingers with his own.

"I don't want to dance." I muttered, but was glad to get the opportunity to see the face of my tormentor.

Shit!!! Fucking masked party!!
It didn't matter. I could do the maths on the cut of his jib just by looking at him: he was tall, six foot four by my estimation, rugby player physique and the most piercing honey-coloured eyes.
My vagina did a samba and went, without question, into his arms as he pulled me close.

"I thought we were going to the dance floor?"

What a stupid question, but I needed to say something to keep me grounded in this insanity as we fast-walked past the dance floor, through a doorway at the end of the bar and into a small dark office.

"This is more private."

His arms surrounded me and I could feel not just the hard on now pressed against the lower part of my stomach, but also every rock hard muscle enveloping me in a grip that had me wanting to throw him over my shoulders and take him to the nearest hotel room and have my wicked way.

Why was I thinking like this? What the hell was making me want to fuck the brains out of this guy?

I was so lost in thought over my feelings I did not realise what was happening 'til I felt his hand push my silk thong aside and dive into my wet pussy.

"Liar," he breathed against my neck.

I looked 'round the side of him to see if we were being watched but everyone seemed to be watching my father strip in the middle of the dance floor to Beyoncé's Single Ladies.

He delved deeper as he kicked the door closed and I moaned uncontrollably with my head falling back and my arms wrapping tightly around him. His hand came out and I felt juices running down my leg.

He raised his hand to my nose.

"Can you smell that Nadia? That is your pussy juice running down my hand; do you want to taste it?" the stranger said.

I wrinkled my nose at the thought.

"What? You've never tasted your own pussy juice Nadia?" He smiled. "Taste it!"

I couldn't believe how much I wanted to reach out and lick his fingers glistening with my juice.

"Come on Nadia, taste it. Taste what I will taste when I suck your pussy. Share the taste of your cum with me."

He pushed his fingers towards my mouth and I wrapped my lips around them. The salty but sweet taste of my own essence, exploded in a hybrid of flavours against my virgin tongue.

"That's a good girl, lick it all off. Are you hungry baby? Do you want me to feed you?"

I moaned my acceptance. What was happening to me? I had become someone I would be utterly disgusted with like my half-sister Charlotte; married and unhappy.

She married so young and threw away her education to be with a damn fool. I had sacrificed everything to get my education, set up her businesses and here I was about to risk it by messing around with this sexy beast of a man.

I slowly began to withdraw my mouth from his hand, this had to stop and it would stop now.

I looked up into his eyes, gathering myself while I delved into the depths of my soul for the sharp focused business-like persona that had got me all I had today.

Opening my mouth to tell him I was walking away, he grabbed my ass again, spun me around so his back was to the party, spread my cheeks from under my skirt and thrust his fingers into my pussy.

No nicety.

I cried out as his other hand pushed my face onto his chest to muffle the sound. He worked his fingers faster and I knew there was no way I would get away without exploding in his hand. He moved me further back against the wall so I was resting against it and he no longer needed to support me. He moved his thumb quickly across my clit as he worked three other fingers into my greedy pussy.

I came fast, silently biting down on my bottom lip to prevent me from crying out. He worked me hard, making the orgasm go on and on 'til I felt limp and my legs could no longer support me. With my breath on its way back, he grabbed my hand and we were off on another adventure, but the not knowing who the hell he was increased the turn on.

Through a series of doors and stairs, we were now away from the party, in another room which was empty.

He grabbed a chair and pulled it next to me so I could sit down, making sure I was not sitting on my skirt or I would have a large damp patch that would be difficult to explain.

I looked up and came face-to-face with a pecan-coloured penis with pre-cum glistening on the tip and, just as I had imagined, I could see a scattering of dark curls peeking out through the zip. I did not hesitate or think twice before wrapping my lips around its wide girth and deep-throating that caramel flavoured cock. It tasted salty as if he had been working up a sweat but I loved it and let my mouth open wide to take him in as far as I could.

I found that spot at the base of his cock that I knew would be my secret weapon, I could not make this last too long, because we could get caught any second now.

He looked like a brother who liked to control his shit!
He should not have picked me.

I used my free hand to grab on his ball sacks. Not squeezing, just balancing them in the palm of my hand. I placed my thumb at the base of his cock, on my secret place and increased the pressure of my mouth as I took him in.
I sucked harder making him slowly near that place of no u-turn. There was no sound because I knew he was trying to look casual. Then I bit down on his hood gently, squeezed his balls hard and pressed on the secret location and then deep-throated him. He jerked and I knew it was over so I increased the pressure and he bucked as he came in my mouth.
I took it all in, swallowed it all, not to let anything linger or things could get messy.

I sucked him clean then tucked his cock away back into his trousers and zipped him closed before standing up. Knowing, by his breathing, how affected he was by what had just happened; he was still trying to play cool, calm and collected.
Yes, I was back in control of this situation.
I am the queen bitch around here.

I lifted my hand and pushed his mask up, so I could see his face. It was a gorgeous face just as I had thought it would be.
"Osvaldo" he replied to my unspoken question.
"Huh?"
"My name is Osvaldo."
"Nice name where's it from?"
"Puerto Rico, or so my mother tells me."
"Cool, well, Osvaldo, meet me in my car in 10 minutes; I'll be at the front of the restaurant. I want you to give me that pussy licking you promised. I'll be waiting."

He smiled a gorgeous, slippery, heart stopping number that made me almost flood my already wet thongs. I walked past him, grabbed my bag and still vibrating phone and headed to the ladies for a much needed clean up and cool down.

20 minutes later I was sitting in my car drumming my fingers against the steering wheel and starting to feel like I got stood up. I felt angry and disgusted with myself for my behaviour.
My phone buzzed again.

"What Justin?" I almost screamed into the car when the phone system picked up.
"I just thought you'd like to hear a friendly voice baby, I know how worked up you felt about seeing your family again."

"I'm sorry baby! It's just been... a manic evening." I calmed down, realising that it wasn't Justin I was pissed off with.

"I thought it would be, well hang in there," Justin said, attempting to be reassuring.

"No, I'm done; I'm on my way home now."

I took one last longing look at the entrance.

I still wanted Osvaldo to fuck me with his huge cock. I was, as they say, gagging for it.

But a smart woman knows when she's been played.

Who the fuck did he think he was treating me this way?

Does he know who I am?

Turning the car off, I grabbed my handbag, told Justin I would call him back, slammed the door behind me and stamped once more into the dark interior of The Cherry Bar, fuming.

No one made a fool of me.

Absolutely no one.

Back at the Party...

Walking with a serious strut, leakage between her thighs and anger painted across her face, Nadia swung through the doors and scanned the room for him.
She knew he was still here.
Fucking Osvaldo.
Nadia was suddenly enveloped from the back as Nia danced behind her, spilling drink on the floor.
"Where you been miss ting-a-ling?" Nia asked, swaying gently. "OI DJ, PLAY SOME SHABBA!"
"I had to get something from the car," Nadia said, still scanning the room.
Charlotte came into view from the bar with a colourful cocktail which she handed to Nadia.
"You okay sis? You look pissed off?"
"I'm... erm..." Nadia sighed heavily, and then took the drink. "I had a bit of a headache but it's gone now."
"Dancefloor ladies?" Nia said, staring into the distance of the bar.
"Who you looking for? You been neck craning all night, who you a look for gyal?" Charlotte asked.
"I thought I saw my work colleague here... anyway, come we go ladies..."
"Um hmm..."

Interlocking arms, Nadia, Charlotte and Nia made their way to the dancefloor, where masked uncles, aunties, grandparents and grandchildren were dancing freely.
From the middle of the threesome, Nia spun Charlotte around, and then turned to do the same to Nadia, who giggled uncontrollably.
   The music suddenly went dead and the DJ patted the microphone and the crowd groaned in unison.
"Sorry for the pause, but the man of the hour would like to say a few words."
"If he's sober enough," someone shouted from the crowd.
   Uncle Franklin drunkenly two-stepped to the stage, his clothes in disarray as a spotlight fell on him. He swayed on his feet as he faced the crowd, trying to block the light with his drink.
"ANYWAY, hello everybody..."
"Hello Uncle Franklin..." the crowd said back.
"Okay," he giggled. "I wanna, I wanna say thanks to ever...

everybodies for coming..."
Nadia looked across at Charlotte and mouthed the words, 'that's YOUR dad acting like a drunk fool'. Charlotte gave him back.

"... you're all lovely, really... and it's nice to see family again. Especially my lovely baby daughter Charlotte. WHERE'S CHARLOTTE?"

Hearing her name, Charlotte froze as everyone turned to her. She managed a well-practiced grin and waved at the stage, hoping the response and wave would be enough.

"COME UP HERE SWEETHEART... I WANNA I WANNA... SAY SOMETHING WORDS..."
He held the microphone in his mouth and held his arms out to her. She tried to wave it off with a fake smile until Nadia began a round of applause in her direction.
Nia followed suit and soon enough, the crowd pushed her to the stage, with Nadia and Nia front and centre.

That was fun, Nadia thought.

"YOU TOO NADIA..." Franklin said. "I want my daughter the business woman up heres with me...
"Shit," Nadia mumbled to Nia as she raised a smile and hit the stage.
With one daughter under each arm, Franklin held his drink high and started to cry with Nadia holding the mic.
"Look... I know it's my birthday... and I'm happy, but I... I just thank the Lord for all of you..."
"WE LOVE YOU UNCLE FRANKLIN." A child shouted from the masked crowd.
"And I love you too... but, seriously... I wanted... my... my girls here... 'cuz I love 'em... they're my little chiccas..."
In the front row, Nia could feel her phone vibrating in her pocket. She checked the display and saw her mum was calling.
She tried to make her way through the crowd but they had filled the room to hear Uncle Franklin's address. Trapped, she crouched down and plugged her ear with her finger.

"You okay mum?"
"Yes sweetheart, Eastenders just finished, I just wanted to find out if your okay."
"I'm fine ma, just at Nadia and Charlotte's dad's family reunion/ birthday party... I think..."

"I LOVE MY FAMILY SO MUCH, ALL OF YOU... ALL OF YOU..."
Franklin's drink rained close to Nia on the phone, with Nadia and Charlotte cringing under their dad's drunken sway.
"I wasn't always... I wasn't always this lucky... I was raised in a really small, dangerous town... and... and... my mum was really really hard and... this is really hard to say..."
"JUST SAY IT," the crowd of masks said and roared to life. "SAY IT SAY IT SAY IT..."

Quietening the crowd, Franklin sighed.
"In my younger days, my name wasn't Franklin, my mama made me change it when I was 21. She said no one would hire, or trust, a man with a name like Alfredo Demarcus, so I became Franklin..."

"What, WHO said that NAME?" Nia's mum asked over the phone.
"Who said what?"
"That name... who just said that name?"
"What name? Alfredo Demarcus?"
"Yes... who said that name?"
"Uncle Franklin."
"WHO?" Marie shouted.
"It's Nadia and Charlotte's dad Franklin. He's on stage giving a speech... mum? Mum? HELLO?"
"Does he have a scar under his right eye? Sort of looks like the tip of a high heel?"
"Yeah?!"
"That man... OH GOD... that fucking man..."

Nia could hear her mum crying over the phone and she hated to see or hear her mother cry.
"Mum, what's going on?"
"I really wished this day would never come... that prick ALFREDO or Franklin, whoever he is with the high heel mark under his right eye – that I gave him – is the man who I unfortunately know as your father."

"...I've made my mistakes in life and when I have the chance to change them, I... I do... because life is short and I wanna go into... into... into... old... age with my family around me."
Nadia and Charlotte were fake yawning as the crowd cheered

and applauded and Franklin unwrapped himself from the girls and walked to the side of the stage.
Nia was now standing up straight with confusion, distress and fear painted all over her demeanour, while holding the phone to her ear. She was looking from Franklin to Nadia to Charlotte, tears slowly filling her eyes.
Nadia caught Charlotte onto Nia's worrying look. They tried to get her attention, but she was somewhere else in her mind and was looking straight through them.
Nadia and Charlotte crouched down to comfort Nia, who was visibly shaking.
"What's wrong babe?" Charlotte asked first.
"I... mum are you sure?"
"What's going on?" asked Nadia.

Franklin dragged a strong, pecan-coloured presence in between Nadia and Charlotte and put his arms around all three.
Their attention was focussed on the visibly upset Nia, who was fully crying as they tried to comfort her.
"Family, I'd like you to meet, welcome and give all your love to Alfredo Osvaldo Demarcus, he's my son."

Foot Soles & Pantyhoes

Tatiana Blue was her.
Five foot nine in flats and six foot four in heels.
Oh the heels.

Caramel topped with a honey glaze, Halle Berry bob of short locks with a blue streak across her fringe.
Draped in a shape-hugging skirt suit, she definitely looked the part.
Today was the day she was making a change.
No more gambling with her life, no more stealing, bye bye to the seedy leather underworld of which she was known as a queen.
Tatiana was no longer content with spending time forever on the hunt for the perfect shoe for her ever growing collection.

She wanted more.
More from life.
She wanted quiet nights in arguing over the TV with a partner; she wanted a family, she even wanted white picket fences.
Deep down, she knew her need for change was rooted in her desire to have children. With her biological clock ticking and her soul craving and broody, Tatiana was changing for a future she despised for so long.
Her heart longed for normality but, with as many shoes as she had in her possession, that always felt like a pipe dream. Sort of like the nightmare her sex life had become.
Stolen moments with random guys scratched an itch but wasn't the cream she needed to heal.
Rather than taking the time to go out and meet someone who could be the yang to her crazy yin, she travelled the world.
Stealing shoes.

The second bedroom in her apartment had become her storage room; prepped for her next move and stacked floor to ceiling in shoes, but hidden to the naked eye.
Alphabetically, and in the order they were procured, Tatiana shelved her shoes in a neat, almost OCD fashion in draws, her wardrobe, under her bed and generally out of sight.
Italy, Spain, Bulgaria, Switzerland, London's West End, Colorado, Las Vegas, wherever designer shoes were made, she was there and made sure that she got what she went for.
Louboutin suede buckle sandals from the factory with lax

security in Spain, Marni satin bow slingbacks from the Prime Minister of Italy's wife with her open bedroom window, Roberto Cavalli lace up leather wedges from Roberto's 'secret' Switzerland getaway.

DKNY, Jimmy Choo, Alaïa, Chloë, Emilio Pucci, Lanvin, Valentino, Charlotte Olympia, Alexander McQueen, Brian Stood, Bottega Veneta and Michael Kors were some of the names in her collection that made her the best designer shoe thief in the world.

Or so she believed.

Tatiana found it an adventure to pick the lock on a Reed Krakoff factory and have free reign over whatever shoes she wanted. There was an orgasm almost every time she turned on the lights and the shoes shined back at her.

Her favourite orgasm was black high-heeled shiny shoes with strong heels.

With over 1,538 pairs of designer shoes in her collection, Tatiana was ready to give it all up in order to make a change.

That meant no more stealing, but she could keep what she already had.

In her head, that was just good sense.

Standing across the road from the office of the Ebony Times, Tatiana could feel herself shaking.

Nervous at the idea of getting the job and being called a fashion consultant.

It was a weird feeling for her considering, just last week, she balanced herself on the wooden beams of the ceiling of Jimmy Choo's China factory with no rope and security looking for her below.

A 'walk in the park' she called it.

Clip clopping with confidence in her Brian Stood all black heels, Tatiana stopped at the crossing, looking both ways before skipping across the street.

She was ready.

She felt positive about her interview and her heart was pumping excitedly then she realised that, for the first time in a long time, she was tool-less.

No lock picker disguised as her mascara, no safe breaker hidden in her blush compact and no retractable heels for quick movement.

For the excitement fiend that was Tatiana Blue, this was the first day of a new day.
And the plan looked good and golden until...

Hold on, let ME tell the rest of this story because this Oh guy won't get it right.
Who better than the man himself to break it down so it can forever be broken?

Hi, hello, what's up, wgwarn, what's good, what's crackalacking?
My name is Russell Reed and, as you were about to find out, I'm the one that "apparently" fucked up Miss Blue's day.
Would I agree with that statement? No, no, hell fucking no.
She just happened to be in the right place at the right time for me. Doing what I do, its all about right place, right time, quick moments, in out, no drama.
Anyway, I'll tell you the situation then you tell me if I fucked up her day, deal?

Okay, so... oh yeah, she was crossing the road. And that was when I saw her. I was following one Greek PH and...

What's a PH I hear you ask?
How rude of me not to formally introduce myself.
My name is Russell Reed and I'm an upskirt addict.
I LOVE that shit.
I walk around with up to three hidden cameras and I film up women's skirts. Nothing sexier than watching a woman's ass and thighs when she walks. But from beneath her skirt. Oooh, I'm telling you, the thought is making me hard right now...

A PH is a PantyHoe, that's what I call my ladies that I film. It's not calling the woman a hoe, its just 'cuz it sounds like pantihose. And I do like pantihose. And pop socks and tights and knee high socks and suspenders, all that shit.
I mean, think about it, a woman's legs are sexy in themselves but, in motion, divine. Then there's the panties.
The best part.
Upskirts work for me because of the panties. Especially on a

nice ass, trust me, I'll be spitting on my hand and wanking out a 30 minute nut to that kinda clip on repeat. If she's going commando, 10 minutes.

Say what you want about upskirt clip makers, 'oh, its illegal' or whatever but the way I've got the camera in my shoes and trainers, you'd never know.

I'm probably filming up your skirt right now. 'Cuz, like I said, I LOVE that shit. I've got over 4,000 DAYS worth of footage. Not hours.... DAYS...

That's your skirt, your friend's skirt, your mum's skirt, your aunty's skirt, the pastor's wife's skirt, your cousin's skirt, your friend's skirt, THAT skirt...

So, anyway, where was I?

Oh yeah, I was in Chelsea, recording one thick-thighed Greek-looking PH who was giving me good footage on my trainer cam. I had another camera securely pointing up in a Primark bag I carried as my primary camera and that was when I saw Tatiana half-skipping across the road.

She was just... slippery.

Made me want to get naked and rub myself in vegetable oil in front of a slideshow of upskirts.

Hands down, the sexiest upskirt I could ever wish to have. And I've had a lot.

I left the Greek and I was onto her so quick. Barging people, stepping on shoes, not giving a fuck. I just wanted to see what she had under that skirt.

The closer I got, the better she looked. From a distance her shape looked promising but from 30 yards, my dick woke up. That was always a sign of a good PH.

She stopped in front of a huge building and that was when I knew I could get her. A risky move but doable.

Filming up women's skirts isn't easy you know!?

I came from behind as she fiddled with her iPhone and it was as if I could see through her clothes the way her skin radiated. Caramac neck tattooed with something that disappeared beneath her shirt and jacket. Her skirt was fitted and formed tight to her thighs. Usually a problem for us upskirters because women tend to walk with less freedom in a tight skirt.

More of a restrained sexy walk.

But a woman in a flowing thigh length dress will walk free as a bird.

The thing with Tatiana, was the way she stood. She stood like someone was taking her picture. One leg was straight for support and the other was out to the right.

And she had these shoes. These black, shiny, smooth high heels on. Her foot didn't look stressed in the shoe, it was just cool.

I don't have a shoe fetish really but I did like those shoes on her. They made her calves look good. That would make for a good lead up to her panties and probably good thighs.

Quick check I was recording and I moved to within three feet of her back. She was lost in something on her phone because she didn't feel my presence behind her.

I checked my BlackBerry, which received a live feed from the bag cam. I positioned the bag between her thighs and swayed so the bag moved forward between her slightly parted legs.

Her inner thighs were stronger than the skirt showed. The backside was... well IS, just a feat of magic. Trust me, if you ever get a chance to fuck Tatiana Blue, take a moment to just marvel at her shape. It's a beautiful thing.

She had on what looked like boy shorts... but they were these black French knickers and they were sitting high on her cheeks.

I slid my foot cam forward for a second shot and that's when it all went downhill.

Out of the blue, she began the 'my phone is falling to floor, let me save it' dance.

She two stepped as her phone fell out of her hands.

I mean, come on, really? That happens JUST as I get a good shot?

She slapped her phone to one hand, passed it to the other and fumbled in between as she knocked it up into the air.

I didn't see the phone coming my way, I was too busy following Tatiana as her thighs separated as she reached for the phone. Brilliant footage though.

It's like God knocked the phone out of her hand to help me out.

Before I knew it, my girl was facing me with her hands high in the air.

It was like slow motion.

By the time I looked up, her phone fell straight into my bag at the same time I heard a loud crack.

I didn't want it to be the camera, I prayed it wasn't the camera as she knocked the wind out of me and pushed me to the floor.

In my whole history of doing this, never once has that happened. I mean what are the odds of that shit?

My phone goes flying, my bag cracks again as it hit the floor and Tatiana's weight forces me down fast and my head even faster. My head hit the ground so hard, I bit down on my tongue. The last thing I remember about that moment was lying on the pavement, looking at my camera sprawled out next to Tatiana's iPhone.

For some reason, the camera had gone from recording to playing.

Through my blurred vision, I could see the camera was playing footage of her. The walk up and the first peek between her thighs. The darkness of the unknown that lurks under every skirt or dress.

I'm telling you, I LOVE that shit.

What I didn't love was the fact I could feel myself losing consciousness. My vision of the screen was deteriorating but, even worse, I could just about make out Tatiana's face as she made her way to her feet. I wish I could've lost consciousness before I saw her face when she picked up her phone then my camera.

I don't know if I said 'oh shit' before I fell asleep on the pavement but I thought it.

I could've sworn I was taken to a hospital because I DO remember hearing doctors talking and that beep beep beep noise those machines make. Like, right by my head.

For the life of me, I remember talking to a doctor, leaving the hospital and getting into a cab. God knows how the fuck I ended up back at home.

As I slowly found full consciousness, I could see I was sitting in the living room on my computer chair, which was weird because I had sofas so I never put that chair in the living room.

My blinds were drawn and the only light came from a small lamp on my book shelf.

The back of my head was pounding, my eyes were watering and there was an acidic taste in the back of my throat. I went to massage my eyes, throat and head in that order but my arms weren't obeying orders. They stayed held together at the wrists by, what felt like, cruise ship rope.

Looking down, there was rope everywhere; draped across my chest and my legs and my arms were linked to the chair.

Something in the back of my head, besides a big ass coco, made me think, 'where's the camera bag?'

This was the definition of a 'what the fuck' moment because when I tried to stand up, my feet were also forced to disobey.

I was strapped the fuck down.

And that was when I could hear something in the distance of my flat. A noise I knew all too well.

Wind blowing, constant rustling, random voices, car horns blowing.

It was one of my videos.

From the sound of it, whoever strapped me to the chair was watching my work. A part of me hoped they were impressed with my sheer body of work.

In the state I was in, I was still proud. Wouldn't you be?

If you'd pulled off some of the shots I had, you'd feel the same way.

My pride wasn't fully erect because I was bucket ass nekkid and tied to my own chair like a terrorist in 24.

Like, seriously, I DID start to panic. I mean, I didn't remember how I got home, which meant someone brought me home. Which meant this person had to be strong enough to carry me up my stairs.

Looking in the direction of my computer room, I listened for any sign of gender. A man's groan or a woman's whimper. Maybe even a ringtone. SOMETHING.

Who the fuck brought me home? Not only home, but went on to further tie me to a fucking chair.

I was so pissed off, who the fuck ties people to chairs anymore?

By this point, I started to breathe heavily, looking around the room, trying to find something to give me a chance against whoever was currently scanning my collection. And if they found the collection, I prayed they wouldn't keep searching.

Shiiiiiit, the worst thing they could do was keep looking. Particularly my external hard drive.

Suddenly, silence.

The sound of the video ending made me shush my own thoughts. Like the person could hear me thinking from the other room.
That was also the moment I noticed that my hardwood floor was covered in a 10x10 clear plastic sheet.
I watch Dexter too so I know what time it is when the plastic sheet comes out.
Seeing it under the chair, my sofas pushed back, a nice little space, made me super fucking nervous.

Obviously, I was shitting myself by now.
I mean who else has such crease-less plastic sheeting like this except for workmen or crazy ass serial killers?
My eyes were looking for anything I could grab and hide as a possible stabbing weapon but I wasn't going anywhere.
On that day, of ALL days, I was not in the mood to be tortured or killed.
But the sheet was hypnotic. It was like I could already see my blood spattered across it.

Another familiar sound drew my attention. Programs on my computer were shutting down. I could hear MSN closing and Skype going through a forced close. The giant of a man who brought me here to kill me was about to get busy on me.

"I'll be out in a minute," a woman's voice said.

HUH?

My mind was screaming, 'NO FUCKING WAY'.
I knew that voice.
I'd heard it before.
Once in the flesh but many times digitally. The inflections of her voice were sweeter than technology could translate.

The light in my computer room turned off and I stared at the door, honestly a little scared at what might come out. The closed door cracked open a little and a sliver of darkness stared back at me.

I knew she was there.

I could feel her watching me, reading what I was thinking, trying to plan an eventuality to whatever I was planning.

Tatiana Blue stepped out of the room as graceful as a ballerina. All she did was walk out and close the door behind her but I was already dumbstruck.

80% was fear, 19% was thinking how good her sex would be and 1% hoped she didn't find anything ELSE on the computer.

With just enough light to see her silhouette, Tatiana's heels clapped towards me.

A part of me was slightly more scared of her than if she had in fact been a tall Russian wrestling-sized dude with no neck.

She walked in and out of the darkness as her heels made me follow her path. She was obviously going for drama as she walked in and out of light beams from the lamp.

It was working because I was sweating like Janine Butcher in confession. The ropes around my nakedness were getting itchy and my dick was suffering the most.

Fucking Tatiana was turning me on and all she was doing was walking around me.

She stepped onto the plastic sheet and the light hit her fully for the first time.

I tried to think about Boris Johnson's knees in the hope that my erection would instantly droop. But Tatiana grinned a pure cane sugar smile that monkey wrenched my train of thought. My dick betrayed me.

"Russell Reed!" she said.

"Yes. And you are?" I replied, keeping the civility going.

She laughed sweetly, "You don't know me?"

I looked her up and down, continuing the dumb display.

Really I just wanted to take her all in. She wasn't wearing the business suit that she knocked me out in. She was sultry. And I don't say that word everyday.

Skin fitted long sleeve, black.

Leggings, black.

Heels, a new pair of black with blue bows.

I looked back to her face, "Should I know you?"

"You're the connect that fucked me over on that shipment of Choos... don't worry, I remember YOU."

Believe me, you have no idea how happy I was to hear her say that. I don't know who this connect was but she thought I was him.

More importantly, she didn't think I was me.

"Connect? I'm sorry, I REALLY have no idea what your talking about. What the hell are Choos?"

I think I pulled sincere off. Her sweet but sinful smile dropped and she came closer to my face.

Standing on my left side, her thigh pressed against my shoulder, she pulled my head back and pointed her iPhone at me.

I flinched because I thought it was a gun.

Anyone would flinch, it was semi-dark, I just saw something silver coming towards me.

It made her laugh.

I felt like a bitch.

At that moment, I was happy for her to think I killed Archie just as long as she left.

Now wouldn't that be a turn up for the books? Would've been the first time ever.

Tatiana tapped away and pulled some screens across her phone and a light shone in my eye. I squinted hard as she spun my head in a full circle, humming approvingly of my neck. I don't know what she was looking for but I know there was nothing there.

"Nothing there," Tatiana said behind my ear.

I froze.

Her hands showed no love as she checked behind both my ears then held my face into the phone light.

"What are you looking for?" I asked.

Then, she came over all confused, like she wasn't sure where she was.

She let my face go, dragging her nails across my cheeks and staring into my drowsy eyes.

"I think I've got the wrong person." she said.

Fucking result.
She bought it.

Which meant she only found the videos and not the folders within folders with four passwords I spent hours setting up.

If she thought she had the wrong place, she'd leave.

My best chance of getting her out was to try and appeal to her better nature.

If she had one.

"Please, I don't know who you think I am, but I'm not him, I swear. I just like to make videos."

"Oh yeah, I can see that... got yourself quite a collection there haven't you?"

I was staring her dead in the eye.

Even in the dim light, I felt like the white boy with the burger in Pulp Fiction.

Her honeycomb eyes were scanning me, looking for a reaction. I was looking for the same, still thinking about the secrets hidden on my external hard drive.

Suddenly, she swirled in her heels, walked over to a long black trenchcoat and slipped it on.

This was another what the fuck moment for me.

Was she leaving?

Was she gonna untie me?

Was the plastic sheeting just to make me shit myself?

"I'm sorry Russell. I've got the wrong person. I am so so sorry."

For the first and only time during our whole interaction, I saw remorse shine on her face. Her eyes softened and she bit her lower lip while looking me up and down. She looked really sorry.

And I felt bad for her. Even though I was the one still tied to a chair.

Then she turned around and left.

Just walked out the door. Closed it, click and everything.

Relief was a fucking understatement.

My body started shaking at being so happy. I let my head drop and took a deep breath. I knew the next mission was to get out of the chair, but I just wanted to... you know... take a moment.

If the plastic sheet was there to scare me, it really did. From what I've seen on TV, you don't think to bring that type of something unless you plan to really fuck up someone's soul.

I didn't THINK she would kill me but, again, that plastic sheet fucked with me.

Leaning forward, trying to create some slack in the ropes, I looked for the closest table.

On my dark oak coffee table centrepiece, I saw an envelope with my name on it.

Large, Manila, A3 size.

I turned my head to try and see my name clearly and that was when my testicular intuition told me that someone was standing at my front door.

You know that feeling when you know someone's about to knock on your door? It was that.

I stared, waiting for the knock. I hoped it was the cavalry. I was willing to take the stick for the roped up predicament I was in.

But if it was Tatiana returning to do some damage for whatever reason, she was locked out.

My front door automatically double locks.

The presence was still there. I could feel them. I haven't got super powers but I could FEEL them.

The door knob rattled for a second then went silent.

Then I heard a little scratching noise at the door. Sounded like a mouse was scratching at the lock.

From my still bucket nekkid seat, dick scratching against the ropes around my waist, all I could do was watch.

As tense as that moment was, I couldn't tell you why I was getting hard. It was kinda uncomfortable because my dick managed to slip through a gap in the ropes.

Felt like I was masturbating with sandpaper gloves and bleach lube.

I was annoyed but the scratching at the door made the lock click once and my attention was back on that.

Is someone picking my fucking lock?

The door opened and Tatiana Blue walked back in with a bag on her shoulder and a smile on her face.

"I forgot an envelope. You haven't seen it have you?"

I was mouth open.

I paid good fucking money for that lock and she had it beaten in seconds.

She WAS as good as they said.

Her walk was more seductive this time than when she left. There was a glide in her slide.

In all black, with the long coat, she looked good.

She picked up the envelope and looked at me with a...
I don't know WHAT kind of smile it was.
It was somewhere between bi-polar and 'I just found a winning lottery ticket'.
"Wanna know what's in this here envelope?"
"Am I in any position to say no?"
She looked down at my dick and her smiled dropped.
It was that moment right there that Tatiana Blue showed me just how absolutely crazy she was.
Clever, but definitely crazy.

Watching her flick the envelope between her fingers, I felt sweat drip down my side. She was enjoying watching me squirm.
"You SURE you wanna know? You're not gonna like it." she said playfully.
"I haven't been too fond of where I woke up so just keep the bad news coming. What's in it?"
Me and my big fat mouth.

"Good question. I was hoping you'd say that."
In my defence of what happens next, I'd like it to be known that I tried.

Her bag fell to the floor first, followed by her coat.
"Well, Mr Russell Adrian Reed, son of Marcia and Marvin Reed, in this envelope is something that, as I said, you're not gonna like."
Did she just full name me? She knows mum and dad's names.

OH SHIT... she found it.
Because of what I do, I don't have my name and information out there for all and sundry. It's only in one particular place.
Work.

Tatiana spoke while she reached into her bag. I watched her every movement, still confused as to why she left and came back. The plastic sheet looked back at me and I turned my head.
More mind fucked than ever.
"In this envelope is everything you've worked for. Your life's work. Dead. In a few simple pictures. I don't know how you found the time what with all your 'other' work."

Sweat was killing me and making the ropes an itchy bitch. My eyes were still scanning the room for something with a sharp edge. I didn't realise my sly eyes were being watched.

"Dont worry Russ, I've moved everything so we can have an uninterrupted conversation"

"I'm not saying shit to you," I said defiantly.

If she was going to kill me, I wasn't going out like a bitch. No way Jose.

But my defiance made her smile curl as she pulled out a bag from her bag.

She held the envelope and a drawstring JD Sports bag in both hands and shuffled on her high heels.

She was having the time of her life being able to tease me. Knowing what she knew probably made her want to fuck with me that little bit more.

But I was trained, techniques in conflict resolution, avoidance, how to disarm using conversation, the basics.

The choice of the envelope or the bag was a tough one. My name instantly drew my attention but the introduction of the bag was a new ting.

"What's in the bag?" I asked, sweat running down my chocolate bald head

"Another good question, Russ is two for two so far. Go for three and I just might let you see it."

"See what?"

That sounded like the introduction of a second entity.

"Patience double R, all in good time."

"Is this a game to you?" I asked. Honestly, I was starting to get pissed off. Who the fuck did she think she was?

"Yeah kinda. Not my usual kinda game but I am having fun. Don't worry, you'll be having fun soon."

The way she said that didn't make me feel good in my stomach.

The envelope slapped to the floor and she reached into the bag, her eyes locked on mine.

It all unravelled from here...

"Do you like music Russell? I loooove music. I'm a soul chick deep down. You like soul don't you Russ?"

My eyes were dead. Not giving her any satisfaction. It didn't matter, her smile told me she was up up and away right now. Didn't bode well for me ultimately.

"Yeah, I prefer old..."

"...school, yeah, I saw on your iTunes, you have a lot of old music. Me, I like the new boys."

Out of the bag came a folded white A-line skirt and a new pair of high heels in a large clear freezer bag.

"I don't care really..."

"Awwww, don't be like that... play with me at least."

She smiled one Keri Hilson grin that disarmed me straight away.

I was hot, bothered, annoyed and I just wanted her to get on with it, whatever IT was.

I couldn't get to my panic button or my phone... shit, I didn't even know where they were. Hadn't seen them since I licked up my head.

"Fuck you Blue," I said. And I meant that shit.

"Oh you will, don't worry about that. One way or another you will."

Stepping out of her heels, she dropped back to her five nine original height. I was amazed at how tall she appeared to be, what pretty feet she had and how thick her calves were.

Really I needed to get out of the chair but she was very distracting in all black.

"Look, what do you want from me? Just hurry up with it and get the fuck out..."

"Oooooooo, a little touchy are we?"

"You already left, why come back?"

"Patience double R..."

Her calmness was working my first, second, third, last and reserved nerves.

She smiled again. This time more sinister than the last.

"If you know my name, then you know who I am and you know there's gonna be consequences for what you're doing."

"That's what the envelope is for... ooooh, I almost forgot my music..."

Her hands sat on her hips as she looked me up and down. Well, more down than up as she slid her iPhone between her leggings and her hip.

The elastic snap made me jump.

I couldn't tell you why I was so nervous.
Well I could, that damn plastic.

"I think we need some Trey Songz..." she said. "Set the mood."
"Just let me go, you know they're gonna be here soon."
"Oh I know exactly when THEY will get here... I've got all the time in the world."

Out of her bag, Tatiana pulled out a speaker dock for her iPhone and placed it at my feet.

I was thinking to myself, why are you watching her do this? Get the fuck out of this situation.

Did I? No. Could I, really? Probably not. Were the hairs on my testicles getting caught on the ropes and itching like Tyrone Biggums? Definitely.

But I didn't want her to watch me squirm. Whatever she was going to do, I wasn't giving her any joy from my pain.

"Are you gonna let me go?" I asked with every ounce of deadpan I could muster.

"Erm, no."

"Tatiana BLUE? Are you gonna let me go?"

"I JUST said no, what makes you think I'm gonna change my mind just because you know my name? Try again double R."

Some random generic R&B tune popped out of the speakers and filled the room. More annoyance on top of my pissed-off'ness.

It was time to do something drastic, see how far she was willing to go.

I took a deep breath while some whiny voiced yout' started singing about how HE invented sex. Arrogant prick.

"HELLLLLP!" I shouted at the top of my voice.

I didn't think anyone would hear and neither did she as she just... watched me. Didn't move towards me to stop my noise or anything like that. She just waited for me to run out of breath, which I did. But that was okay, I had plenty more where that came from.

Taking in another deep breath, I prepared an even louder shout.

Then she slapped me.
The bitch slapped me. With the back of her hand too.

That shocked me and made me super pissed at the same time.

"Get me out of this chair right now, do you fucking hear me?"

"How can I hear my music with you making all that fucking noise? Shut ya mouth."

Tatiana looked down at me like I was crazy. She started the song again and stood in front of me, still holding the skirt and her freezer bag heels.

"Ready?" she asked me.

Was I ready to get out of the chair? Quick, fast and in a hurry.

"Are you gonna let me go?"

Tatiana kissed her teeth. "You're ready..."

She did not mean ready to get out of the chair.

With the music and light creating an atmosphere I couldn't ignore, Tatiana swayed her hips to the music in a silent ting all her own. She was no longer looking me up and down, her eyes were closed. It wasn't like she had to watch me. I wasn't going anywhere.

"You know what Russell, I was not telling the truth before. I DID have the right man. I'm a little fibber."

"If you are not going to let me go, then we have nothing more to say to each other. So like I said before, and 'cuz it had a nice ring to it, I'll say it again. Fuck you Blue."

"Someone get a little slap feel all emasculated?" she asked teasingly.

I don't know if she was trying to annoy me for a reason but she was good at it. Which annoyed me even more because I was supposed to be the one in charge.

"How 'bout we do it your way then? Or at least, the way you like to record it."

Her hands slipped to her hips, fingers seductively massaging her skin as she looked me in my vex eyes.

Her thumbs hooked into the elastic of her leggings and pulled them down with the beat of the song.

"You know what Russ, I've gotta give you props. You hid that stuff on your computer real REAL well..."

My eyes were, of course, stuck on two of the finest, muscular caramel legs I've ever seen. I actually started to think if I, somehow, got out of this, one of my first ports of call was the full upskirt video of Tatiana Blue.

She reached her ankles, bending from the hip, not the knees, like a good girl. Of course I was thinking of fucking her from the back. Look how she bent over, all flexible and shit.

Obviously for effect.

I didn't care. On the outside.

Inside, and down below, I was bubbling nicely.

The tail end of a six-pack snuck out from beneath her black top and sat over a pair of black lace French knickers with a picture of a high heel on the front. She stepped out of her leggings, looked down at her shoes then looked at me, getting right back to conversation.

"When I first looked, I didn't see it but I looked again and... oh, silly me, I forgot about the envelope."

Honestly, so did I. It slapped to the floor what seemed like ages ago.

She bent to pick it up, showing me my name.

"This, mate, is what they call insurance. See, after I found the... what did you call it? STUFF? I had to make sure that I covered my own back. So I went home, got some things and got to work on you."

My face must've looked like I smelled shit and sardines because, again, she succeeded in messing with my head.

I didn't know what was going on. What had she done to me? When had she done it? When?

"Whoa, wait a minute..." I broke my unspoken vow of silence. "When did you 'get to work'?"

Upright and lording over me, she smirked. "Well, I brought you back Sunday, went home Tuesday..."

"What FUCKING day is it today?"

"Friday I think."

Now, this, was some real bullshit. How the fuck had she managed to KEEP me here and I couldn't remember it? And for a week, didn't anyone miss me?

"That's not the worst part," she added. "What'd you think I could've done to you in that time?"

Here's me in one big bitch of a predicament and she goes and puts that in my head.

"See, when you saw me on Friday, I was on my way..."

"What the fuck? Are you a fucking kidnapper as well as a thief?"

She slapped me again, this time open palm forehand. Heavier and more forceful than before.

I REALLY couldn't tell you how pissed I was at that moment. Those slaps had some real venom in 'em and with my arms strapped by my side, I couldn't even defend myself or shake her the way I wanted to.

I had to watch the slap coming.

When my eyes eventually opened, keeping the anger under intense lock and key, she held a blue polished finger nail in my face.

"Stop interrupting me, its pissing me off."

"Your slapping me and you think YOUR pissed off?"

That was apparently the worst thing I could've said. The look on her face told me that something in my last sentence had seriously pissed her the fuck off.

"You know what, fuck the skirt bit. You've pissed me off now. I WAS gonna treat you a bit but you FUCKED it all up with your fucking talking."

I really had set something off. Her calm demeanour during this whole exchange was light and breezy up until now.

The song changed at my feet and the same whiny prick from the last song came up, yodeling like an idiot.

In front of me, she was pulling her top over her head. The frantic anger she displayed as she threw her top onto the sofa did not make me feel any better.

She worked OUT that's for damn sure.

I caught myself staring, her slender creamy caramelness was not bad to have to stare at.

Reaching back for her bra clasp, she paused to look at me.

"You don't deserve Lauryn and Aretha 'cuz you pissed me off."

'Unusuaaaaal' whined the iPhone.

Tatiana closed her eyes and took in a deep breath. Raising her hands to her chest plate, she held it.

Whatever was going to happen was going down now and

after all that slapping shit, she best do me something because I WOULD get out.

And God help her when I did.

Didn't have much time to think about getting out because she finally exhaled. And opened VERY evil eyes at me.

One look at her heels. She moved to them, slowly.

Her left foot slipped in and the weirdest thing happened.

The heel disappeared and she was suddenly wearing a flat shoe. I thought it was fatigue fucking with me until she slipped her right foot in and the same thing.

Didn't know there was such thing as a collapsible high heeled shoe.

Then the funniest shit happened.

Looking up at me from her ankles, she pressed her thumb and forefinger on her left earring and, I swear to you, she grew.

No fucking joke, she grew.

I know my mouth was open because its open now just thinking about it.

Hydraulic heels.

"Nice heels," I said.

The legend of Tatiana Blue was apparently very true.

She went to over six foot three in her heels.

Standing well over me and grinning almost maniacally, Tatiana was breathing like it was her last breathe.

Then she calmed.

The music at my feet changed to a song where the whiny voice sang about being successful.

Annoying because I could not see a successful way out of my current predicament.

"I know everything about you Russell. Everything. I know who you are, I know what you do."

"So you know the best thing is to let me go don't you Blue?"

THIRD SLAP...

This time, to really humiliate me, she slapped me once with her forehand and followed the same path with an eye-opening back hand.

Etiquette, old school training and my profession went out the window and I really wanted to fuck this woman up.

I'm tied to a chair and she gave me three clean connecting slaps. Of course I wanted to kill her.

"Early in the week, I thought about letting you go, but then I started investigating and that was when I found your STUFF on your computer."

I thought I was hallucinating because the angry Tatiana that looked like she was about to lose it was replaced by this swaying to the music, starting to smile version.

My guard was up just in case she wanted to raise her hand to me again.

There was something about seeing a slap coming from a woman that is just so offensive to me.

"I don't know how you do it," she said. "Its like leading two lives. Anyway, after I found that stuff, I realised I was in a bit of fix. 'Cuz I could understand how SOME may class this as kidnapping, so I had to think outside the box."

"Whatever." I replied, indignant.

"Trust me, this is the bit you should be listening to. When you ran into me, or I ran into you, do you know where I was going? I was going to a job interview. That day was supposed to be the first day of my new life. But you and your fucking camera had to fuck it up. And now here we are."

My head dropped and I spoke in a hushed tone. "You can still fix this, just let me go."

"No way Reedy, I've already had to go through this, your only awake for the end of it. I would've explained all that but, being a man, you pissed me off and lost the privilege, so now we're just gonna do this."

"End of what? Do what?" I asked, sweating like Smokey in Deebo's pigeon coup.

Tatiana hooked her thumbs into her Frenchies and pulled them down to her metal heels.

In my head I was thinking, so this is what we're doing?

"When I said I know everything, I meant everything. Good to see you passed your last STD test. That's the type of specimen I've been looking for."

Now I don't know why the hell this happened. Even telling you now, I still don't know why my dick got hard when she said that. Maybe it was her tone and the way it felt like death was in the air.

After the second slap, my erection shrunk with my growing anger and was nestled uncomfortably between a gap in the ropes.

But he was now up at the prospect of sex.

Traitor.

"Bang me if you want but you know how this game is gonna end."

"Not if I change the rules."

Her first contact with my dick was a soft one. Her warm hand encircled me and worked a slow deliberate rhythm.

"Tatiana... look..."

"That's the first time I've heard you say my name in the sexy way it deserves. Just for that..."

She opened her mouth and a long line of saliva landed on my helmet and disappeared between her busy fingers.

"Sleeping me with won't get you out of this?"

"Not true."

Her slippery hand was starting to feel real positive but I tried to ignore the pleasure with random thoughts. What's gonna happen after I come? Why isn't she telling me anything?

I felt like I shouldn't have pissed her off earlier.

"Tatiana Blue, that's your name isn't it?" I repeated.

"Yes IT is!" she replied with a deep sigh.

Hearing her name was the key for her to open the door. She stepped out of her knickers that were bunched around her ankles and swung a leg over my thighs.

I gasped because she did it so swiftly. I wasn't ready for it.

We'd been so far apart for so long, I wasn't ready to be so close to her. My face was still burning from her slaps but, again, my dick was responding to her.

He's a slave to closeness.

I was breathing real heavy because I had no freaking idea what she was thinking. Maybe she wanted to say bye in a nice way. Who knows.

I certainly didn't.

Smelling of an intoxicating perfume and the odd taste I had in the back of my throat when I woke up, Tatiana held my face and looked into my eyes, with her hand still making me wince in pleasure.

"Don't worry Russ, this isn't the first time I've done this. Although this is the first time you've been awake."

"WHAT THE FU..."

Before I could get the expletive out, Tatiana raised herself up and slipped down on my dick with no ceremony.

It was a total pleasure shock to me but she took it the worst. Her locks were whipping about her face as her head and back arched.

This was one of those moments when this whole situation didn't feel so bad. Watching Tatiana arch in my lap while her amazingly wet pussy slid tightly around my dick was one of the highlights. Her hips slid from the left to the right and her legs raised until there was nowhere for me to go but up and in.

We both sucked air through our teeth. I wanted to run my hands over her arched front, a soft hand between her caramel breasts would've made the moment that little bit sweeter.

Only thing I could massage was rope and chair wood.

This was not how I saw this going.

Me fucking Tatiana Blue.

Tut tut tut.

But the pussy was worth it.

I don't know how pussy can be sweet but it was juicy fruit. All that slapping must've made her wet because she was dripping through the ropes across my thighs.

Back on an upright riding axis, Tatiana ran her nails across my bald head.

Not a light sexy drag, that shit hurt.

She could see she was hurting me but as I frowned, she dragged her nails deeper.

Could've been her way of distracting me as her inner walls squeezed my dick. She lifted herself and released with a slow drop.

I may have looked a picture of restraint but I was struggling.

To have good pussy thrown on you is one thing but to not be able to touch, to feel, to rub a nipple... it was killing me.

My fingers were moving as if they were free to roam.

But they, like the rest of me, was forced to watch.

"How lucky were you to run into me? Huh? Tell me Russell?"

Her lips hovered so damn close to mine, I jerked forward, hungry for it. Holding my face strong in her neck, she dropped her head and moaned. A progressive, climbing to a mountain top moan. I could tell she was going to come. Her walls were throbbing and she was breathing faster.

"You know this is rape don't you?" I said, trying to ruin her orgasm.

Breathlessly she replied, "You've never once told me to stop."

And then she came.

She held my face up in her hands and kept riding me on a wave of four orgasms, one after the other. Her hips were jerking with no sort of rhythm and she held my mouth open as if she was stealing my breath.

In her eyes was pure pleasure.

Being able to take what she wanted and forcing me to watch her do it was sweeting her up nicely.

Up and down stairs.

"Happy now?" I said sarcastically. I had to act like I didn't enjoy it.

"Whew... AM I? Look at this face... can I kiss you Russell?"

I was quite shocked by the question. Considering what she was doing and her method of doing it, she had no problem doing whatever the fuck she wanted.

But to ask for a kiss, something quite personal.

Tatiana licked her lips just inches from my dry mouth.

She was waiting.

Her pussy was catching its own breath as she throbbed on me.

"You kidnap me, hold me hostage, do whatever weird shit you did to me THEN ask if you can kiss me? Knowing who I am, you don't think that's taking the piss a little bit?"

ANOTHER QUICK FOREHAND SLAP.

"STOP FUCKING HITTING ME!" I yelled.

"Or what?" she replied, grinding her hips with her question.

I had a reply, started with F and finished with K but her movement was too good a feeling.

It was a good thing I couldn't touch her otherwise I would've rammed myself deep inside her.

Her slow, slick, dragging move was driving me up the fucking wall. I wanted her to let go of my face but she wanted to see what she was doing to me.

"Fuck you Blue... this won't change anything."

SLAP. BACKHAND.

"Yes it will... Oh God it will... this dick changes EVERYTHING..."

Oh... how I wished she didn't keep slapping me. They were some real face turning claps and my face was sizzling. Not to mention I was already hot from being so fucking frustrated.

And she chose that moment to start riding me with expert precision.

"This... won't... change..." I tried to say.

She grabbed my face and snarled at me as if she was transforming into something. Then she grinned in a way that worried me.

I was right to worry.

She licked my face.
Top to bottom, chin to forehead.
"Just one kiss. Please?"

Tatiana's hips were hovering on a medium heat as she awaited my answer. Smelling nothing but her minty saliva across my face, I was getting to an emotional point of exhaustion and a sexual point of orgasm.

"Stop. If I give you a kiss, will you let me go?"

She looked at her Mickey Mouse watch, "If you kiss me, I won't have to."

"Huh?" Her fucking cryptic answers were more than doing my head in.

Grabbing my jaw strongly, Tatiana looked in my mouth. She was breathing normally and was feeling a new groove on the medium heat.

Her lips were so close, we were breathing for each other.

I'd never had the urge to fuck and fight at the same time before. Quite a mind fuck actually.

"Oh Russell... you could've been something special..."

Her lips were soft and cautious. I opened my eyes because it felt like she was shaking. And she was.

Two solo tears fell from her eyes.
I didn't expect that.

She growled in the kiss.

The salt from her tears crept into our kiss and softened her lips. She sucked my lips as if it had been a long time since she'd felt such a feeling.

I wished for a different distraction tactic because her medium heat was bubbling up to a high temperature.

Tatiana had my face cupped in her hands, blocking out the world around us.

She was flicking her waist good and hard, making my dick stab deep inside her. My head rubbed against something smooth and circular inside her and made my sensitive helmet harden.

"Don't do this... Tatiana..." I said, struggling to fight such beautiful movement.

"I have to. And I kinda want to..."

I would've given up my whole career just to be able to touch her face, feel the warmth of her back, tap her clit at the moment of orgasm.

Her nipples were in my line of sight, getting harder before my eyes.

"Wish you could touch me don't you?" Tatiana asked, breathlessly.

"I..."

My mind sent the sentence to my lips but the words never made it.

I was being rained on and I knew if she kept moving the slippery way she was, I would come.

One of her hands left my face and felt my heartbeat.

"You LIKE that don't you?"

"Shush..." I answered. Her sexy voice, after her moist lips left mine, was not helping my resolve.

"Don't you dare shush me, who the fuck do you think you are?"

And there was the attitude switch again.

I moaned a deep, throaty groan and she sat down fully in my lap. The soft button I reached inside her was feeling my helmet and Tatiana's hard grinding hip movement made them kiss harder.

Her frowning face was a picture.

She looked like a spoiled brat who didn't get her way.

"Now you're gonna have to come," she said.

"No, this... this is only gonna make... things worse."

"After that orgasm I had, there is no way this can get worse. Now, shut your mouth and come inside me."

You KNOW that was the beginning of the end for me right?

With her hips looking like they were barely moving, but OH were they moving, she slipped her hand down to the moisture between our groins.

She dipped two fingers in, alongside my dick, then took her scented digits and rubbed them over my lips.

I tried to say no but her hand was quite tasty over my mouth and right under my nose.

"NOW you can come."

Any guy, who can put himself in my situation, knows what happened next.

The moment wasn't helped by her airy, almost sleepy voice in my ear.

Everytime I tried to speak, her taste slipped down my throat and made my hips jerk upwards.

The succulent sensation of her walls getting wetter around me made me beg her to speed up.

But:

1) She wasn't listening to anything I had to say.

2) Her own breathing began to speed up and she started to moan in that familiar way.

I wanted her hand off my mouth so I could moan free and proud. The pussy was THAT good. If things were different and this was a bedroom situation, I know damn sure I'd be screaming like a bitch. Would I care?

Hell no.

"GOOD boy... Tatiana likes that dick where it is...keep... it... there..."

"Stop... please... I'm... gonna..." I mumbled under her hand.

"You're gonna what? Huh? You gonna come?"

Her goading was making the pussy all the more sweeter and I was licking the back of her hand, enjoying the flavour.

I nodded as my tongue tickled her hand and she giggled into a long moan.

She brought us nose-to-nose and her eyes searched mine. Her pussy was sliding over my dick and I clenched my ass. I was trying to hold back but she was rolling herself all over me.

Boooooy, I can't lie, she dropped one sweet swirling stroke on me and I lost it.

So deadly was the grind that I fell instantly silent. My eyes widened and I knew there was nothing I could do.

Slightly uncanny was the fact that Tatiana sped up on my dick just at the right time, drawing my orgasm out.

Inside her, I was slick as grease and her walls were smooth as silk as each descent left a wet line of her travelling down my roped thigh.

I was coming... and not even the return of Jesus could stop me.

Tatiana, reading me again, thumped her hips into my dick so hard the chair rolled backwards.

"You've already done the big... biiiiiiig bit, finish the job."

"Huh?" I mumbled.

"You can't... arrest me if... if... I'm pregnant with... your child can you? That would change things wouldn't it?"

She might as well have just slapped me again when she said that. My eyes were wider, I was trying to Incredible Hulk out of the ropes and, more than anything, I wanted her off me.

All her cryptic answers throughout this whole thing had been about this.

I know I didn't tell you I was police but, come on, you must've guessed.

Well, as an officer of the law, fornicating with criminals is kinda frowned upon and can kinda lose you your job.

Getting someone as sought after as Tatiana Blue pregnant, after mountains of legal red tape and paperwork, was definitely worthy of prison time, regardless of the circumstances.

I mean, imagine trying to explain that Tatiana Blue kidnapped me?

She really chose her moment to drop that one. When I was long on the road of no return. And this one started deep in my balls.

Tatiana swirled her pussy in a circle and whatever fight I had in me shot deep into her.

I came like two buses at once.

I was sweating and could feel myself spurting longer and longer streams of soldiers inside her.

"Whose a good boy?" she asked before closing her eyes and grabbing my jaw.

Tatiana shuddered then froze.

Shivered and froze.

Shook a little then froze.

Screamed, hushed herself then froze.

Her walls did the same.

I was a quivering, shrinking mess. She, on the other hand, was still vibrating in my lap. My nut must've hit something right.

It was after that good feeling washed over me that I truly took in what she said.

"You... you..." I tried to speak as she uncovered my mouth.

"Me... you... Russell Reed and Tatiana Blue... it rhymes."

"Are you fucking crazy?" I asked. "You think sleeping with me will stop me from locking you up? Your a thief, you know we've been following your movements for..."

"But I noticed you had no pictures of me in your STUFF files. See that's how I wanted it. So, the only person who knows who I am is you. And you Russell, have made me pregnant."

The way she kept saying pregnant, like it had already happened was not making me feel good. It still felt like she knew something I didn't.

"Daytime policeman, night time upskirt voyeur huh? So your not adverse to keeping secrets are you Russ?"

And that's when the penny dropped.

This was her plan all along.

Standing up, she looked down at her thigh and the thick trail I was making to her knees. With both hands, she scooped and put them right back where they came from.

I couldn't believe what she was trying to do.

"Tell me being pregnant by you doesn't change things?"

"You know it does. But your not dumb enough to think that this will get you pregnant."

"No," she scoffed. "This was just to say bye. You got me pregnant earlier in the month."

"WHAT? HOW THE FUCK DID I DO THAT"

Sucking a creamy finger she said, "If you hadn't pissed me off before I would've told you everything but you and your fucking smart mouth. Don't worry, the envelope will explain everything."

THE ENVELOPE WITH MY NAME ON IT.

I forgot about that. Considering what just happened, it was understandable.

My eyes shot to it as if it was the doorway to Narnia. What the hell was in that envelope that could explain the unexplainable?

Tatiana bagged her speaker dock and checked her iPhone.

"Uh oh, time to go."

"What? Where are you going?"

"Me?" she replied while slipping her bra straps on and sliding into her knickers and leggings. "I gotta go. No point me being here, besides someone will be here soon to... help you."

"Fuck no, who?"

I was frantic at this point. Who else was about to walk into this pantomime that I was forced to take part in?

"Your cavalry."

Her bag was packed quick time and she was back in her original heels and trenchcoat.

Crossing the plastic sheeting towards me, she checked her phone again.

"Russell baby, I've REALLY gotta go."

"Don't you dare fucking leave me here like this."

Shushing me with a scented finger, Tatiana leaned in and kissed me.

I could've been mistaken but the way she kissed me told me that there was a lot more going on than I knew.

And the answers were in that envelope.

"See you in about nine months."

"WHERE THE FUCK DO YOU THINK YOUR GOING? GET THE FUCK BACK HERE!"

Another slap. Both forehands.

"Stop shouting at me boy, who'd you think I am? Is that how you used to scream at Cherelle?"

My anger at those slaps would've made me go Super Sayain

four if I was free but her last minute name check had me freshly confused.

How the hell did she know about Cherelle?

My ex-wife after seven years of marriage.

Job killed the connection between us. But there was nothing in my file about her.

"I told you, I know EVERYTHING..." she said, sensing my confusion. "I'll call ya... and make sure you get that promotion, we can't raise a child here. Kisses and sexy slippers..."

She kissed her finger and placed it on my lips then turned on her heels and clopped to my front door.

I was sitting there, as I had been, watching her walk. It was more a sashay with a glide. Whatever it was, she was still sexy with it.

Tatiana opened the door as she sprayed her hands with anti-bacterial hand wipe. She ran a tissue over her hands and wiped the doorknob.

"Make sure you get to that envelope before SHE does."

The way she said 'SHE' told me that she really did know everything.

I was in a state of serious 'oh shit'. With our orgasms dripping down my thigh, I had to gather myself and think about:

1) What the hell was in that envelope?

2) If Tatiana really knew everything and SHE was coming, then I had to hide that envelope and come up with a good excuse as to what the hell I was doing like this.

"Your the first man to tell me he likes my shoes."

"Tatiana, don't do this..."

"Everyone wins this way. You finally get the grandkids your parents are harassing you for."

"How do you know all this shit? Your a supposedly pregnant shoe thief on the run from police agencies on three continents, how do you win?"

"If you tell them what happened here, you know what will happen but if you don't, you get to keep your job and our baby gets to have both parents."

"WHAT THE FUCK ARE YOU TALKING ABOUT? YOU'RE NOT PREGNANT, HOW CAN YOU BE? FUCKING UNTIE ME."

Tatiana smirked in the doorway and looked at her feet.
"Good luck explaining this one."
She blew a kiss and was gone in a whisper.

The door slammed and I was all alone.
Again.

After such a drama of a something, the silence of the room was unsettling. I even missed the whiny voiced singer she played at my feet.
But I didn't have time to think about that.
My mind, thoughts and all my energy wanted to know what the hell was in that envelope.
My name stared back at me in thick black letters.
I didn't know what was in it but I wanted to see it on my own. Something in the way Tatiana spoke made me believe every word she put on it.
Teasing me because it was so close but I couldn't reach it.
"AAAAAAHAAAH, COME ON..." I screamed in frustration, trying to wiggle out of the ropes.
Then it all got that little bit more fucked up.

My door buzzed which meant someone was downstairs trying to gain access to the building.
Of all the voices I could hear through the intercom, I was glad to hear my boy and fellow officer Jamal.
"Russell, its me, Jamal... I'm here with Femi and... HER... look, I don't know what's going on but she said she was coming, so get your shit together 'cuz... BLOOD CLART, Femi, look at she in that black coat. Thank you darling... don't worry Russ, some sexy ting in all black just let us in..."

CLICK...

Tatiana actually let them in the building?
For fuck sake.
I looked down at myself, a thin line of blood drawing from a cut on my face and sweat everywhere.
In the chair, I started to rock, trying to tip myself in the direction of the envelope.
It wasn't the greatest idea and I had a feeling it would hurt going down but I had to do something.

Tatiana was right, it WAS gonna be hard to explain what I was doing tied to a chair, naked, with plastic sheeting under me.

I'd get more sympathy if I was down on the ground so it looked as if my captor dumped me and fled.

Tip to the left, roll to the right, tip a bit more, rock a bit right, come on... you can do it...

With enough momentum, I slowly balanced on two wheels for what felt like ages and then toppled.

On my way down, I felt and heard something crack in my wrist and I yelled like a child. Anyone who has ever broken their wrist knows how much it hurts.

I landed with most of my weight on my shoulder which, added to my wrist injury, could be used for a good cover story.

Yeah, I was thinking about a cover story because, for some reason, I believed what Tatiana said.

I didn't even know what day it was. She said something about me getting her pregnant earlier in the month. But she said she'd been here a week.

You can see why I was on my side, in a next kind of pain, trying to scoot the envelope under my sofa before my door opened.

I must've looked like a right knob. I'd fallen and I couldn't get up. But how I'd fallen allowed me to get fingertips to the envelope.

If the three of them took the lift then they should be at my door any...

KNOCK KNOCK KNOCK

"Russell? You in there?"

"Yeah..." I shouted while fumbling with the envelope at the edges of my reach. I couldn't get enough grip on it to give it a good push. "I'm down... I've been tied up..."

"We're coming in," Tara shouted from behind the door. "Jamal, kick the door in."

Oh shit, come on... almost there...

"With pleasure, I've always hated this door," Jamal said, taking his first kick.

GOT IT.

I clamped two fingers on a corner and pulled it into my hand then tossed it with as much momentum as my injured wrist would allow.

I didn't see it but I heard it skip over the plastic just as my front door flew open.

Jamal and Femi were first through the door.

Femi saw me first and rushed to me with a smile.

"Fam, what happened to you? HE'S HERE."

Jamal followed behind and worked with Femi to untie me. They wouldn't believe what happened here, but I had to work on my story because Tara walked through the door after them.

Strong and thick in her six foot one stature, Tara, my chocolate boss, strolled through my shattered door.

Her eyes expressed relief and she smiled at me as Jamal and Femi got me upright.

I looked at the space where I hoped the envelope wasn't. And it wasn't.

Making it to my feet, I used the rough ropes to give my dick a rough rub down.

Yes it did hurt.

"We got the missed call from your phone. When we tried your house phone, it didn't ring and your mobile rang out."

"Are you okay baby?" Tara asked, breaking the rules of our private office relationship. I already told Femi and Jamal what was going on between us, they were my boys, but Tara didn't know they knew.

And her calling me 'baby' in front of other officers was a new place for us.

I guess in the situation, all rules went out the window.

I looked at Tara in her teary eyes and started my story.
What did I tell them?
What was in the envelope?
What happened to Tatiana Blue?
You wouldn't believe me if I told you...
Now, did I ruin her day?

Your Chair

Please... please... please...
Come in
Have a seat
Make yourself comfortable
Now your feet are firmly planted
It's time to give you what you wanted

Deflate and relax
Let's erase some of the stress from your back
A massage then a kiss before a dam collapse
I'm being nice in my description
Of a sexual act
That gets me hot and seriously bothered
Major fact

I want to be your chair
The object that's always there
At work, at home, in the car, at church on Sunday or even right here
No squats for this
Give you thighs a rest
And let me improve your comfort
Let my lengthy cushion benefit from it
Chair in a bank
Leave a deposit
Leave my face shining like precious Onyx
Slam yaself down pon it!
That is what I seek
Someone to sit down every day of the week
Just chair tongue
Bare fun
Setting sun
Calling on
The orgasm you know will come
I'm not afraid of the taste
And no I'm not insane
You've obviously never had candy rain
Make a chair with a hole and investigate
Something as simple as a seat
Make you masturbate
Cry me a river deep
And watch me drown

You'll hear Mary J Blige in your head
The way I'm going down...
Hard of hearing
'Cuz your eyes are rolling
Your thighs are shaking
And my face is tingling
This is addiction
Plain and simple no fiction
Providing you with something to trib on
Dance that reggae winey wine song
GULP

Talking and swallowing,
Not easy you know
Ladies, you know
Hold on to the sides
This is no ride
Stationary
Simply
Face riding
Chin guiding
Don't care if your grinding
Just sit in
Your Chair...

Moody Blue

Her arms were aching, rain was pouring down on her and all she could see was brick in front of her. The sound of traffic and the rain drown out the footsteps of the security guards she was hiding from as she held on to the wall with her contact surface-sticking gloves.

"Just another day in the life," Tatiana said to herself, shaking water from her dreadlocks.

Not that she was scared of heights but she thought better than to look down as she dangled over twenty storeys up from the ledge of the Suchang Trade Company in Hong Kong.

And then it hit!

Shocked her and totally took her by surprise. It always did when it turned on.

Her contact lenses faded her vision to complete black and that meant only one thing. Russell.

Colour drained back into her right eye and she was back in front of the brick wall with rain drops falling over her eyes. Her left eye was seeing something else.

Russell Reed was backing through his front door with a woman stuck to his face in a passionate kiss. He kicked the door closed as his hands ran up and down the back of the thick woman in a terribly short dress.

"Who the fuck is this bitch?" Tatiana said, spitting rain water from her mouth.

Here she was thinking about and providing for their future and there he was, being a whore. Granted, she had yet to tell him that they had a future together but that still didn't mean he could whore around with any and everyone.

"Especially some tramp with a terrible weave."

With her gloves holding fixed to the wall, Tatiana was forced to watch them in her left eye as they grabbed at each other's clothes, spinning through the hallway in a passionate kiss and there was nothing she could do about it.

She knew what she was feeling though. She was angry. She was more than angry. She was livid.

"Oh Russell... trust me... I'm the only pussy you're getting!"

Russell and his companion were crashing against walls, discarding clothes and leaving a trail of them from the front door. From the hidden cameras she left around his flat, she was getting the best shots of a film she didn't want to see or could do anything about.

Her arms were aching for stretching for so long and she could feel the rain seeping through her clothes. Her spandex t-shirt and leggings were sticking to her skin and water droplets were dripping into her eyes.

"The things I do for a fucking pair of Loubous," she said, peeking into the window where two security guards were looking at the boxes that she knocked over as she climbed out of the window.

"CALL QUINCY!"

Tatiana heard her phone begin to dial in her handsfree earpiece as she was forced to watch Russell back into his bedroom and push the woman down on the bed with a smile.

"Hello?" Quincy answered with sleep in his voice.

"It's me."

"You? D'you know what fucking time it is?"

"Yeah I do, why do you?"

"Always with the jokes Blue. What'd you want?"

"I need a fire alarm with sprinklers please."

"Geez, what trouble are you in now?"

Tatiana focussed on her left eye and could see that the mystery woman now had Russell on his back and was standing over him while pulling a t-shirt over her head and unclasping her bra.

She couldn't help the anger that was rolling through her; all she knew was that Russell was hers, she was coming back for him and there was no random woman in the world who would ruin that.

The sound of the window opening stole her attention and she began to walk her hands across the wall. The gloves were holding fine, though the rain was making her nervous as Quincy said the only problem they have sticking to surfaces is in the rain.

"I'm not IN to anything. I just need a fire alarm and a sprinkler malfunction."

"Where?"
Tatiana told him.
"But that's..."
"I know."

"But why would you..."

Russell and his companion were both naked and laying on top of each other, sharing a passionate kiss and enjoying the feeling of each other's skin.

With no audio coming through, Tatiana was forced to watch a silent version of events with the torrential rain distracting her senses and making it so that she couldn't concentrate.

"Ready when you are!"

"Thanks Q, give me 10 mins then boom."

"Done and done."

She looked up at the window again. There was no one there.

Slowly, she scaled the wet brick wall and looked in through the window to find that the security had left the room. She unlocked the window and began to climb in as Russell was slipping on a condom.

"Fuck that!" Tatiana said to herself as she lifted herself onto the window frame.

"You ready for it?" Quincy said in her ear.

"Do it NOW!"

With both legs swinging into the office, Tatiana crouched behind a desk and watched her left eye, waiting.

The woman was bending over his bed and spreading her cheeks while he manoeuvred himself behind her.

The first splash of water dropped before the fire alarm went off and it hit Russell in the middle of his forehead. He looked up just in time to see the rest of the water fall from the ceiling. The fire alarm followed.

"YES!" Tatiana screamed. "GET YOUR OWN MAN BITCH!"

She watched as the woman scrambled out of the room to avoid the cascading water which was falling throughout his flat. She was picking clothes off the floor as Russell was chasing behind her getting his own clothes on.

"Happy now?" Quincy asked.

"I'm out of the rain and my man is inside in the rain so I'm good."

"Okay, good. I'm done. I'm going back to bed. Don't call me unless it's life or death."

"Don't worry," Tatiana said, stuffing pairs of Christian

Louboutin black lace suede clic booties into her side sachel. "I'll be back to see Russell in person real soon."

This Is Not The End, This Is The Beginning...

Made in the USA
Charleston, SC
26 March 2016